ALEX WANTS
TO CALL IT LOVE

SILVIA SANZA

*Library of Congress Catalog Card Number:*90-64193

British Library Cataloguing in Publication Data
Sanza, Silvia
  Alex wants to call it love
  I. Title   II. Series
  813.54[F]

  ISBN 1-85242-214-9

First published 1991 by
Serpent's Tail, 4 Blackstock Mews, London N4

Set in 11/13½pt Bodoni by AKM Associates (UK) Ltd, Southall, London

Printed on acid-free paper by
Nørhaven A/S, Viborg, Denmark

For Roger

CHAPTER ONE

I didn't get a good look at her
but I'd know her if I saw her again

On Christmas night it was three degrees out. Nobody's car could start and through the creaky windows of his third floor apartment the sound Martin Worthy kept hearing was a motor trying to turn over.

Some words came back to him from an article on salsa in the *Soho Weekly News* years ago: A life is nothing but a string of memorable nights. 'I'll buy that,' he said to himself out loud with a smile that faltered. He did not know why he was even going to the Christmas party when what he really wanted was to be with his eleven-year-old Elsa. But she was out in Jersey with her aunt in one of those places where the cars couldn't start.

He picked up the t.v. guide thinking that maybe what he really wanted to do this Christmas night was stay home. *Lilies of the Field* (1963) was on Channel Five and Channel S at the same time. Channel N offered *On the Waterfront* and the t.v. listing had it as two words, WATER FRONT. A movie called *Rollover* was on; another called *Dragonslayer*. And *A Day For Thanks on Walton's Mountain* (1982). *Ah! Wilderness* with Lionel Barrymore (1935) was on and that would have done it, but he'd have to wait until midnight. So, all in all, Christmas

night on t.v. was even less promising than Christmas
night off t.v. The party, he thought, with a sigh. I am not
a performer, I do not like crowds.

He fumbled around the scramble of papers on his
desk for the party directions and realized it was only a
few blocks away. It was ten o'clock at night and he felt
Christmas closing in on him.

Kate and Teddy, the couple who were giving the
party, had been together for eight years. They kept
talking marriage but never got around to it. They wore
wedding bands anyway, thin gold circles from Broadway
near Chambers. They had really been out looking for
hibachis at Odd Lot but ended up going into a jewelry
store instead.

The living room, where the party was being held, was
a square that could be called spacious although it was
not huge. Behind glass doors, tiny panes and gauze
curtains, two smaller rooms opened off it. The walls
were painted lemon, the ceiling turquoise, and the
woodwork a color called Parchment from Martin's Paint
Stores.

These two people lived varied days and full lives and
used memories to decorate: a painting from a vacation in
Haiti, two red and yellow tigers, side by side, one with
his mouth wide open, the other placid, their tails
blending together into a man-eating desert plant. A felt
banner 'I Love The Sullivan County Catskills' because
that's where they wanted to buy an old farmhouse. On
the wall was a multi-colored kite they called Phoenix
Rising and somewhere next to that a black and white
poster of a ballerina dressed like a flapper. A little
higher, a small watercolor one of their friends did of
Louis XIV coming out of a birthday cake.

Against one wall was a stately walnut chest of drawers

well over one hundred years old that his aunt had given them.

On the wall opposite the chest of drawers was a large desk. Narrow wooden shelves with glass doors lined the top part and held a variety of books: *Skeleton Crew* by Stephen King and *Johnny Got His Gun* by Dalton Trumbo were right there in front. The latest addition was a small book they picked up at a church auction in Jeffersonville, New York. It had been published at 50 Walker Street, New York, 1863. It was called *Bradbury's Golden Chain of Sabbath School Melodies* and had the words and music to songs with names like 'Deeds of Kindness', 'Cross and Crown', 'The Evergreen Shore', and 'I Will Be Good, Dear Mother'. The bottom part of the desk folded closed so no one could see what was inside. Here's some of what was there: a matchbook cover from Federico's ('a trattoria'); an ad from the Sunday *New York Times* Real Estate section, 'Nine room farmhouse, Ben Franklin stove, one and a half baths, rocking chair porch, six acres with fruit trees and berry bushes, nice views, $89,900.' There was a pocket calculator, an envelope addressed to their insurance agent at Allstate, a fat yellow pen that said 'Know the consequences of driving drunk or drugged—New York Department of Transportation, Edward I. Koch, Mayor,' a sales slip from Woolworths for $17, and a clipping from the *Voice*, 'Are you Overweight? Only one visit necessary,' about a patented and trademarked method of hypnosis.

But their favorite piece was a simple small straight legged table that was just the right height for everything. They had picked it up years ago at United House-wreckers when nobody else had discovered the treasures to be found there. It stood in front of the sofa in their first apartment which had been a small one room; three apartments and one coast-to-coast later it was still here.

The square living room could hold twenty comfortably but every year more than that came because all year long the host and hostess told people about their annual Christmas party and somewhere in September they seriously started collecting types and extending invitations. Indeed, they collected people the way they did furniture: nothing matched but everything belonged.

When Martin arrived at the party he slipped into a shadow and looked around thinking, 'I was designed in the forties. I'm like a bridge ready to crack, a bridge only other people get to travel on.' He was weary with the intimacy of the landscape, bored with the over-educated who like to believe they are in control while they get more jittery all the time. He stood planted in one corner and watched people bow and lunge. A female voice: 'I can drive but not good enough for a car.' Across the room he saw the back of a boy with a wine-colored satin jacket embroidered with the word 'JAPAN' and dripping with dragons. He caught sight of a redhead. The boy with the satin jacket, Alex Chase, turned around and caught sight of the redhead too, thinking, 'She's really not that pretty. You have to catch her eyes at just the right time and then maybe you just might take a second look.' But the sad glow of patience on the redhead's face made Alex keep looking. The redhead was sculptural—tall, shapely, coordinated and vulnerable. She was gentle but dark.

Martin Worthy was feeling vaguely uncomfortable but perfectly fine, looking over freshly painted walls and corners to latch onto. Being alone is the only way I have control over everything, he was thinking. This was a thought that had never come to him before and he did not understand where it had come from. Perhaps it was a combination of things, the dry mild boring laughter crowding the room, or his third glass of hot mulled red wine, the sugar, cinnamon and sliced oranges going to his head. He heard someone behind him say, 'Hypocrisy is built into democracy,' and a countering remark, 'I don't know about that; all I know is when those Spanish men look at you, you know they mean business.' And the girl who made that remark moved in one graceful turn toward Martin Worthy and focused her eyes with rigorous finality on the glass of wine in his hand.

'Were you here when Teddy was trying to light that wine so he could serve it flaming but he never got the flame to take?' She had straw colored curls for hair and went right on talking. 'I had about six glasses of that so far,' she smiled. And in a confidential tone: 'This isn't one of my best Christmases. I was so depressed I had to get stoned just to write out my Christmas cards. And this year the Christmas seals and the Christmas stamps both had faces of Santa Claus on them. After a while everything started looking the same and I didn't realize I was taking blocks of four postage stamps and smearing them over the back flaps of the envelopes and using them like they were Christmas seals. So when I went to put the postage on, there were no stamps left.'

And a man across from them had a big artichoke and was peeling off the leaves, snacking on them, giggling about the fuzz, and exclaiming, 'Finally, finally, you get to the heart and hold it in your hand.'

The girl with the straw colored curls, Kathryn, known as Kary, grimaced. She looked like a high speed shining angel. Wired. A simple idea in its most advanced form. Not too beautiful but adorable. She had boisterous eyes. 'Oh, God, did you hear that, get to the hearrrrt and hold it in your hannnnd.' She lowered her voice just a fraction. 'He's a lawyer,' she said with a knowing nod of her head. 'They can kill you with their cleverness.'

'All I know about lawyers is all the ones I meet have a favorite restaurant in Chinatown, usually off on a side street, like "on Doyer off Pell"; and it always specializes in dumplings. Then you get to know the guy better and you find it's really his father's favorite restaurant because he doesn't have what it takes to find one to call his own.'

Kary could only smile.

A cat leaped up out of nowhere, bruising the air, and landing on the edge of a planter.

'I can remember all the names of my friends' cats but I can never remember what name goes with what cat,' Kary said. 'And what makes it worse is that everyone has more than one cat. Jill has three and I can never remember who's Rocky, who's Bambu and who's Max. And Timmy has Amos and Eli, which are boys' names for girl cats. And Annie has Tiger and Snow, and my nephew has two cats, Fluffy and Midnight, and even they confuse me. Why do you think that is?' She did not wait for an answer. 'I think it's because I wish they were dogs. When I was young, my friends and I all had dogs. Then you grow up and everyone moves to the city and has cats. But it's funny how I can still remember all the names of my friends' dogs. Frances Conway had a Dalmatian called Captain and Ellen Delaney had an Irish setter called Shannon.'

'Why don't you get a dog then?' he said, feeling he had to say something.

Kary waited only a minute. 'Too much trouble,' she said.

Someone was discussing the chickens that were about

to be served, each one weighing about eight pounds and called, appropriately enough, an oven stuffer. No one knew how to carve them, though, because chickens were rarely hefty enough to require carving. But, said Teddy, if you knew the anatomy of a chicken, it shouldn't make any difference how big or small it was. And Kate added, 'Put another way, if you know the anatomy of a fowl, a chicken should be built just like a turkey.' And together they, host and hostess, tackled the job. The chickens were delicious and the ham was too, and if you were listening, you would have heard someone say it was hard to believe the ham came out of a can.

The music changed and took the room with it. Kary, whirling away, said, 'It's noise but it works.'

David Pond, the lawyer, was across the room trying to forget that he was going bald. Life was rather empty and it showed on his face. At thirty-eight he had been to bed with no more than five women, one of whom was his wife. Mrs David Pond was even further across the room than her husband, thinking about wrinkles and wondering if it was true that the less you smiled, the slower the wrinkles came.

On his way out, not too much later, Martin Worthy realized he was trying to live in what he had begun to call the order of importance, struggling to keep it all straight. He nodded a parting smile at the girl who couldn't remember the names of her friends' cats. She was talking to the girl with the red hair whose back was to him, and who was saying, 'I don't know what it was that I wanted this Christmas, but I know I didn't get it.' Martin walked down the two flights of stairs thinking, 'Sometimes death is jeopardy and sometimes it is compromise.' He had no idea where these words came from or what they were about. Three blocks later nearing the subway station he remembered that the boy in the satin jacket was the same kid who had been in the poetry class he had taken at St Mark's Poetry Project.

Back at the party Fiarette, the girl with the red hair, watched a young man coming towards her; the front of his wine colored silk jacket was decorated with delicate pink and blue oriental flowers. Alex Chase, lanky, thoughtful, mournful, moving slow, was in his late twenties. If you took the time to watch his face, he could get sad before your eyes. Alex, hard to read, boyish, tentative, aloof, appealing. Clean shaven, baby faced, a solo project with tabloid appeal. A t-shirt that said, 'Help me, I'm trapped inside a human body,' expressed precisely what he suffered, but he would feel like a jerk wearing a t-shirt that said anything on it at all. What made Alex Alex was not what he did do, but what he did not do, would not do. He would never wear an earring, nor a shirt with an alligator on it. He liked to wear suspenders and plaid shirts rolled up to the elbows. His hair was very brown, thick and curly, and a haircut never cost him more than five dollars. He had a Mick Jagger mouth and loved Bob Dylan. He longed to be a classic and, ultimately, a classic example, but he went through life hallucinating. He heard lines in his head like 'The moon has no sister; the moon has no status,' things that he thought would make great songs.

    Alex had finally decided to get closer to Fiarette. One long step before he reached her, he began talking. 'Everyone's been saying how much they like my jacket all night so I thought I'd come over and see what you thought of it.'

She smiled in spite of herself. 'Turn around and let me see the whole thing.'

He turned around, slowly, grandly, and she saw JAPAN with those satin multicolored dragons spinning space and slaying it.

'It's very nice,' Fiarette said. She thought it was more than nice.

'Here I was just three blocks away with my friends trying to reheat a turkey on an electric frying pan.' He paused and screwed his face up. 'It doesn't work.' He has good timing, Fiarette was thinking. 'So we ended up coming here. I never know where I'm going until I'm there. It complicates reality.' He paused. 'So what do you feel like talking about next?' Another pause. 'Talking is what keeps me sane.'

She said nothing. Her shoulders were getting heavy; something was starting to happen, she was beginning to notice him.

'Okay,' says Alex Chase, 'let's talk about the moon. Let me tell you a few things about the moon. For one thing, you can depend on it. Here's how it works. It orbits the earth from west to east in 29.53 days and it has phases. You got to find time to think about things like the moon and the sun and the stars. It's like good rock 'n roll—it never goes out of style.' His eyes explained everything.

'I just got a room on Sixteenth Street and Sixth Avenue. Had enough of the family, you know?'

'Do you have any brothers and sisters?'

'Yeah, two.'

'Two what?'

'Sisters.'

'Younger or older?'

'Both older.' A look crossed Alex's face. 'I guess I better tell you about my brother.'

'I thought you said you had two sisters.'

"That's what I have to tell you.' Fiarette looked at him; he couldn't wait to begin. 'I bumped into my brother on the train one night a few months ago and there he was dressed like a girl. He told me to call him Gloria from now on, and not Steve. That's why I think of it as having two sisters. So the night I ran into him he wanted me to go up to his apartment. He showed me pictures of himself in drag and he said, "Don't I have a mean look in these pictures?" You know, I just didn't know what to say. He has a tattoo on his arm, he looks just like a total man to me, and then he starts telling me how he puts plastic on his eyebrows to tone them down when he goes in drag, and how he shaves his arms, his legs and his chest. I asked him if he had any hair left on his body and he told me he doesn't shave his pubic hair because it itches. He told me that the night before he had had a shot of estrogen. He has a friend of his shoot a dose of it into his buns. He says he takes it for skin tone. You know, we grew up in Jersey, not far from Philadelphia. We went to the same high school. My brother was on the wrestling team. I was the one who wrote poems. He went out for a long time with the same girl and everyone thought they'd get married.

'Anyway, I stayed over at his apartment that night and when I woke up I saw that he had red polish on his toenails. Then at breakfast he told me that on Wednesday the rabbi was coming. The rabbi had a sick son at home so he couldn't afford to pay more than twenty dollars. The rabbi would put on a condom at home before he left and when he got to Steve's he never even took his clothes off once. All the rabbi wanted to do was touch Steve's cock and come, clothes on and all. Then the guy would murmur "wonderful" under his breath and leave. After he told me that—that and the toenail polish—I felt sick. My crazy brother laying all that on me. And my parents just had a twenty-fifth anniversary and should have been divorced twenty years ago. Merry Christmas, right?

'My last job was for a company that made manhole covers and related objects. I wasn't around long enough to find out what the related objects were. They told me the name of the company could be found on every manhole cover if I took the time to look. Anyway, I'm not working now, but next summer I'm going down to Maryland and work with my cousin making three-piece lawn furniture sets out of wood. We figure we can make thirty, forty thousand dollars in five months.

'Tell me the name of an old movie,' he urged, 'and I bet I can tell you who acted in it—probably even who directed it.'

Fiarette was looking at him trying to figure out whether or not he was cute.

'What are you? Jewish?' he asked her.

'Scottish.'

'I'm half-Italian and half Romanian-Gypsy. And I know what everybody thinks about gypsies. But we don't steal, you know. As a matter of fact, I relate better to my mother's side of the family, she's the gypsy side—than I do to my father's.

'I never manage to save too much money—it's my emotions. I never have much, but whatever I have I spend. Spending money seems to help define life day by day—it's a deliberate examination of conscience that I do when I'm feeling selfish. Sometimes I play and sing in the Blue Mill Tavern. I was thrown out of two colleges so far—Cortland State and New York Community and I'm thinking of studying marketing at N.Y.U.'

And Alex Chase popped another something into his mouth, the bitterness clipping his tongue, and Fiarette said, 'Why are you so destructive?'

'So you can save me, lady. I'm here to give you something to do.'

Fiarette looked around for Kary who was nowhere to be found because at that moment Kary, a slinky lantern, was saying to someone named Yo Yo, 'You can share my bed tonight if you'd like.'

All at once Fiarette felt her strand of beads snap. She clasped both ends with shaky fingers and picked the necklace slowly away from her throat, the soft pink wooden beads, notched with white, tied with string wearing thin after too many years. She fought a tear from her eye and felt heartbreak. 'These were a gift from my mother,' she said, 'and I don't want anything to happen to them.' She could feel his eyes on her tears.

'It's so much easier to live a life surrounded by things you don't want or don't care much about losing,' Alex Chase said very seriously.

'That's not always the way it works,' she said.

'I know. I just thought I'd give you something to think about.'

When Alex Chase went home that night, the only thing that was cold was his nose. He knew the wind was there but he could not feel it.

CHAPTER TWO

As Patti Smith would say
'Because the night belongs to lovers'

On that all important day after Christmas, when happiness had been unwrapped, stars had been dimmed and tinsel had been tracked, Fiarette sat in her bathtub soaking in three capfuls—one is the recommended quantity—of Crabtree and Evelyn peach kernel foaming bath oil. She wished for two things: bath water that would stay hotter longer and the sound of quiet. The hammering downstairs was driving her crazy but she knew the driving noise was repairing damage she had caused by letting her bathtub overflow into the apartment right under her. Tempted as she was to step out of her cooling bath water and jump on the floor to hasten the silence, she knew better.

The phone rang.

'And what are you doing the day after?' Kary's voice said.

'I was sitting in this damn freezing bath water thinking that every time I have sex lately I end up crying. It isn't what it used to be.'

'What is it then? What else can it be?'

'It's like something that used to be different. Something that lost its touch. It's something sad. A proving ground. It's become lonely.' She was sorry she had brought up the subject.

'So then don't do it,' Kary said off-handedly. 'Maybe you're coming down with the flu.' Over the phone came the sound of a kitchen. And Kary said, 'I'm making a can of Campbell's mushroom barley soup. Simmer means don't let it boil, right?'

Fiarette sort of laughed.

'What about that guy?' Kary asked. 'The one with the satin jacket?'

'Tempting, but not very.'

'But you went home with him, Fee.'

'Not yet.'

'It's just a matter of time.'

'Life is a matter of time. You know, Kary, there's more to life than the next man you go to bed with.'

'That doesn't sound like you.'

'Plus I'm tired of telling guys what to do to improve the quality of their lives.'

'Jesus, where'd you get that line?'

'Who knows where anything I think of comes from these days.'

Fiarette took another bite of her apple and another and another until there was nothing left but a sticky spotty yellowing core. She held what was left in her hand until it got warm and felt like it was growing.

'So, ask me what I ended up doing last night,' Kary prompted.

'Let me think.'

'No, I want to tell you. I met this guy who told me his name was Yo Yo. He was from somewhere in New England and he said there are some New England towns that are threatened, *threatened* by *denim*.'

'And? So? So? And?' Fiarette opened her refrigerator

door and wished she could find some red grapes and caraway studded cheese to go with them.

'And he was going to visit his sister who lives in Buffalo Grove.'

'Where's that?' Fiarette said, as she tossed the apple core across the room into the sink.

'He never told me. He said it like I should know where it was. He did say his sister had big tits so they called her Moo and he was about as close to her as he could get to anyone and she had a temper and got mad as hell but wouldn't hurt a fly.'

'And then? And then?'

'And then and then he came here.'

Silence.

'So, what are you up to?'

'I think maybe Alex might call me about last night.'

'What does he do?'

"Who knows. He probably has a sister in Buffalo Grove.'

But Fiarette had been lying to Kary about Alex. She didn't mean to lie; she wouldn't have called it a lie. Kary was her best friend and sometimes that made it more important to keep things from her than from anyone else. But of course Alex had come home with her and left not too soon afterward. She smiled as she remembered it. 'What are you doing with that?' he had asked her, as she dragged her big terry robe along with her from the bath to the bedroom. 'In case I get cold,' she had said.

'You won't get cold. I promise.'

And he had kept his promise.

Martin Worthy turned on the radio to the end of a

discussion. 'Everyone is sensitive but borderline neurotics are very much so.' The discussion was over and a commercial began. 'I'm just wild about Harrah's and Harrah's wild about me.' He turned it off.

The morning after Christmas the day's mail turned up a copy of *The Cradle of Soaring Cemetery News*. He had been receiving it ever since his wife had died and he had buried her there, his wife who had waited to die in the grey afternoon of a life so full of rain, the kind of rain that doesn't make anything smell fresher or look sharper, but slips the world a cast-off color. The last thing Martin had done for his wife before she died was color her hair. It was a mixture of two shades, one called sparkling burgundy, the other shimmering auburn. He realized too late she wasn't getting rid of her grey for him. He learned that when a man is considering running around, his wife is already at it. We go to war not because of what the other guy did but because we're afraid of what he's going to do. He could not remember now, he realized with minor alarm, whether she had died on May eighth or May twelfth. Love didn't come easy and the absence of life after so dim a life was easy to explain. And now here he was, with a copy of *The Cradle of Soaring Cemetery News*, understanding that death was a change of residence, somebody's deliberate decision, the end of a friendship, the passing of time, quite natural, quite. Men who work and assist at cemeteries and mausoleums are now known as memorial counselors.

This particular issue of the *News* featured a class of schoolchildren from a school in upper Manhattan who had come to tour the vast cemetery grounds; they visited the final resting place of famous people who were buried there and did gravestone rubbings. The children, it said, went home tired but happy.

He looked at the picture of his daughter Elsa on the wall. He had taken it last Halloween when she was getting ready for a neighborhood costume party. Purple leotards, a striped leotard top, purple eyeshadow and a green face which she told him proudly was the result of Noxema and food coloring. He picked up a letter she had started to write to an advice column in *Young Miss* magazine, grateful at least that it wasn't called *Young Ms.* 'Very often after my friend Melissa and I make plans, she changes her mind at the last minute. I've told her how much it bothers me, but she still does it. Is there anything else I can do?' She was growing up; her emotions were making her think. She was already ten pounds overweight.

His loneliness became restlessness, and he decided to take a walk. Just a half block away he met Margie, a very old lady who he knew lived in the neighborhood but he had never known where. She stopped when she saw him and they stood together in the grey afternoon. He was trying to figure out if she had ever been pretty but it was very hard to tell. She had freckles all over where they shouldn't be and her faded blonde hair was the texture of steel wool. She was in the mood to talk about her late husband; holidays did things like that. 'John,' she said grimly, 'I was so lonely after my John died. I would go into my room and cry and cry and my dog would look at me and turn his head to one side and then the other.'

'Did he die long ago?' Martin wanted to know.

'Nineteen years. He was from County Cork and I was from Dublin. We met at a dance. His sister invited me to their home and then my mother invited him to our home and three months later we were married.'

'Did you have any children?'

Her voice was a whisper. 'He couldn't produce them. I think it was his re-ligion. He always had his prayer book open.'

Martin noticed her nose was dirty.

'He worked for the Holy Name Society. When they buried him, I fainted. The priest picked me up. Somebody tried to give me a pill, but I don't take those things.' She stopped for a moment and then started again. 'We met at a dance,' she said, smiling.

And then he knew that yes, once, long ago, she had been a girl and a pretty one at that. Now the flesh hung around her chin and under her eyes and the skin above her lips was pleated. But there was still some twinkle to her eyes.

'You're still a young man,' she told him.

Martin smiled. Young man indeed. He wondered if maybe what with John 'not being able to produce', Margie was still a virgin. He was thinking of his wife and how in those hot early years he could tell by her warm breath on his arm in the morning that she wanted him. He would take his hand and bring it down to just below her belly and let her take it the rest of the way. He came back to now and smiled at the old lady. She had been talking again, something about John's heart attack, his bed, her bed, and the car she sold for two hundred dollars after he died. Martin was thinking about getting an ice cream pop, the creamy old fashioned vanilla one folded in crisp milk chocolate, even though it was the dead of winter.

At home he found Elsa sitting with her headphones on. He was wondering what the hell it was that so fascinated kids with headphones, the way their eyes slipped shut and their hair bounced from side to side, while fingers shredded the air. He wondered what music sounded like so close to your head flat up against your ears like that. Everything seems so hollow, Martin Worthy thought, why does anyone want to listen any harder than he has to? But that was his own private feeling and not to be shared with an eleven year old. Life was starting to get too serious for him, the pushing in his chest, a distance between him and reality; he would take a deep breath and tell himself to stop worrying, a tactic that rarely worked; he wished it was because he was afraid of not succeeding, but he was more afraid of not even wanting to succeed and that was what saddled him with apology. He was haunted but he had trouble putting conflicts into categories. His thoughts paced.

Elsa slipped her headphones off.

'Daddy, one of the first things I want tomorrow is a piece of watermelon.'

'It's a little early for watermelon, you know that.'

'I know that,' she said, with the resignation of having to be grown up. 'Daddy, if you loved someone and they went blind, who do you think would hurt the most, you or them?' Her eyes were wide with waiting for an answer.

'Okay, Elsa, what soap opera did you see that on?'

But her face didn't change. 'Will you be at my bedside when I die?'

'Okay, enough. Who's going blind and dying now that you want to tell me about?'

'Nobody, I just feel afraid. What makes someone stop being afraid?'

He could hear a shiver in her voice.

CHAPTER THREE

You Want to Learn About Romance?
Watch Robert Mitchum

That Christmas night Alex Chase had scratched Fiarette's phone number on the inside cover of *Devil Dolls*, a paperback he had found on the stoop of a building at West Fourth Street and Sheridan Square. For Alex Chase the week before Christmas had been like this: he had been in jail for two nights; well, actually, it was the mental health ward on the first night where they gave him thorazine and the House of D—for detention—on the second night. This was for stealing three books from the A & S department store in Brooklyn, a crime for which he didn't feel at all guilty. Alex Chase loved to read. He loved words. They made up for fickle reveries.

Now it was March and this past week he had almost been thrown out of the rooming house where his mother had gotten him a room to get him out of her hair. This time around it was the landlord who tried to get him out after Alex walked out quite nude onto the street one day, the street being Sixteenth Street between Sixth and Seventh Avenues in Manhattan. He didn't mean anything by it, he tried to explain, he just wasn't thinking; he was in a hurry to make a phone call to Fiarette. That

was a month ago. He had made that phone call and he
had made a lot of phone calls to her since.

'I was so stoned I almost forgot to take my drugs,' Alex
said to Fiarette, trying to get a trickle of a smile out of
her. 'I need all the help I can get in this constant search
to justify my existence.' Alex was always carrying
something. This time he walked into Fiarette's apartment carrying a black binder with a label on it that said
in purple crayon 'Flying Down to Rio'. Inside the binder
were looseleaf papers with lyrics all over them. Alex
wanted to be a songwriter. His smiles dripped at the
corners. 'I like to get stoned,' he told her, 'it brings
everything closer.'

'So, what'd you do so far today?' Fiarette asked him.

'I was in the park selling ups. Now I am not and never
have been a drug dealer. But a good deal's a good deal.
One thousand B/C capsules for seventy-five dollars.
They're what black beauties used to be. I can easy get
three dollars apiece for them. And sometimes girls from
Jersey even go for four. But,' Alex summed up grandly,
'greed is not in my blood. All I want is enough to get a
ticket to New Zealand. I figure being there will help me
to stop being so self-absorbed. Not being self-absorbed
means learning to live with what's around you. It is the
healthy way to go about an orderly life. You miss out on
a lot of misery.' And then he took a deep breath and said,
'What do you think of this as a hook for a song? "I like to
go to church in the rain."'

Fiarette watched him. He had not stopped talking
since he had walked into her apartment, a synthesized
madness. She wondered how many of those B/C caps he
had kept for himself. But she didn't wonder too hard. He
was getting so caught up in her, but she was having none
of it. Her indifference was hardly disguised as lifelessness.

And so this night, like most nights, she let herself walk into his arms and be kissed, hard. And he moved closer to her and the next thing they knew it was morning. The sun was not up and maybe it would never come up. Mornings like that made Alex wonder why he should get out of bed if the sun could choose not to. The first thing he said to her was, 'I went to Ernest Hemingway's house in Key West once. Then I went up to Miami but I didn't like it at all. Too many people getting old.'

His grin was waiflike but it had muscle. He tossed an orange up in the air and caught it on the way down. 'A bolt of citrus flavor,' he said.

Fiarette had started working a few weeks ago at a law firm and even when she was paying attention, which wasn't most of the time, she still didn't understand what was going on. She was learning how to be a word processor. The law firm sent her to school for a week to learn the machine, and right away she was filled with a hard refusal to assume the identity they were shoving down her throat. Perhaps it was working with machines that made her even more possessive of her uniqueness. She did not want to be branded a word processor. And so she fought it all the way. She was a creative soul who couldn't really create anything, but she loved to try. She sat there playing with her hair. Fiarette didn't want ribbons and clips and braids in her hair. She just wanted her hair to be there, a floating performance; long and hot on her neck in summer was when she liked it best; it made other people hot just looking at her and she liked that part, too, the delicate hostility of letting people know the heat didn't bother her.

And so in word processing school when they were having a quiz and the instructor said, 'Fiarette, can you tell me what the CRT is?' she simply said, 'The what?'

David Pond was on her mind. She didn't know it yet, but that's what it was. She was destined for a headstrong fairy tale.

'The CRT.' She knew she had no room in her head for what she didn't want there.

'The CRT,' someone else said.

It started to come to her. The cathode . . . but she couldn't find any more of it and started wondering if the instructor was tricking her by asking her questions about stuff they hadn't even learned yet.

'The cathode ray,' the instructor said grimly, 'it was in yesterday's lesson.'

'I guess I missed that part,' she said, and thought she heard someone laugh.

And all day every day her first week on the machine she made notes, but when she read them back they didn't mean a thing. They sounded like this: 'first format block for col. headings, reg. tab and special tab needed for parameters for code 5.' Something called the alternate shift key made her stop and think but not the way she was supposed to. She wondered if you could really shift yourself into an alternate key or key yourself into an alternate shift.

Machines, she had decided, made her feel mean. She could not remember any time in her life when she had felt so mean. She hated spraying the machine with static guard so the paper wouldn't get caught in the automatic feed of the printer. She hated how when she hit the delete key the prompt line said 'Are you sure?' and how when she made a mistake it said 'Reformat error'.

She was bored by the work, peddling for crumbs, and bored by the people; they erased her head. She wanted to be alone to cushion her survival but when she found herself alone she wanted to bang her head against the wall. She began to find it easier to punish people than to deal with them and to wonder if punishment was the inspired lyric of a penal code that might really work. There seemed to be no right way of doing anything, it was all up for grabs. And none of this was anything like the Fiarette she knew; she was changing before her very eyes, to the applause of the aching ballad.

Today at work she was wondering if those red bumps on both elbows that she kept scratching at until they bled were shingles like Kary said or psoriasis like Alex said. Whatever it was it was starting on the knuckle of the middle finger of her right hand, the ring finger where she never wore rings; they annoyed her. They always felt too big unless they fit right and if they fit right, then they felt tight. They were more trouble than they were worth. If they were expensive like the one her mother had given her, she worried about losing them. If they were cheap, she worried that they looked it, like the silver band with the orange stone she bought in Vera Cruz. Life was not easy. Bare chested calamity. She was thinking about the Universal machines at the gym and decided she would chart her progress. She thought of the article about women bodybuilders in *Psychology Today*. And she was thinking about another article about skin ailments and stress. Psoriasis was not a pretty word. And it was all over her elbows, the right one, the left one, and she scratched at it until it bled. There was even some in her right ear. She liked to think of herself as a survivor and a visionary, but her skin was coming apart to remind her she was mistaken. Her stress was her crippled chanting for unconditional comfort: she wanted to succeed. She wanted to succeed at the everyday tasks of life, like bench pressing fifty-five pounds for one set of ten reps.

On a good day she could do only four or five. And it angered her like a child who tries in vain to take the first step and, not quite ready, stumbles again and again.

Fiarette did not think that what had been was necessarily better than what might be; she camouflaged the shrieks and the blood bath, never doubting that what she had done in the past or been part of could be done bigger and better in the future. But some part of her resisted, fearful that all too complete confidence was akin to defying gravity. We get better at some things but only warm at others. She shook her head and told herself to stop.

She was, she knew, self absorbed and she remembered what Alex had said about self absorbed.

At lunch she sat in the park and read from *Why Meditation?* It said to free yourself from all goals, enlightenment can come only when you are willing to lose your ego. She began to worry about her ego because she knew it caused trouble, bound as it was in the technology of opportunity. Her ego encouraged self-consciousness and the fear of anything permanent: the fears of childhood had shifted but remained grounded in self absorption. She needed a project to absorb her so she could stop absorbing herself.

Growth is its own reward, a subtle but final shift in values. Fiarette was watching and waiting, running out of bullets. She did not care about a thing and this lack of emotion was so out of character for her that she began to wonder who she was.

At night she would go home and fill a page of her journal with her collages. She would cut out of newspapers and magazines things that caught her fancy. Like a headline that said BRIEF ENCOUNTERS. Then she would save a sticker from a drugstore bottle that said

'This prescription cannot be refilled.' It was bright orange with deep black printing and she would stick it under the headline that said BRIEF ENCOUNTERS. Or she would save fortunes from Chinese fortune cookies. 'The restless see today, the patient see eternity.' Or a price tag from a pair of jeans with the original price of $44.99 crossed out and the sale price of $34.99 in green and then in red $25.99 and finally in a brown pen '$19.90', which is where she came in. Or she'd clip a quote in the middle of an article like: 'Order,' said Alfred North Whitehead, 'we must have order . . . but not too much order.' She loved sympathy and vague games.

She went to bed that night and had two dreams. In the first she lived next door to an elderly woman and went over to visit her one day. The neighbor had company, another old woman who introduced herself by saying, 'My name is Heaven.' Fiarette said, 'That sounds like a midwestern name.'

The second dream was about David Pond, a lawyer she was becoming infatuated with at work. He was married but she didn't want to marry him; she wanted only to kiss him up and down.

The next morning she didn't remember either one of her dreams, but they were there, wherever it is that dreams go on their way to moving into morning.

CHAPTER FOUR

I don't have much to say about what it is that I do.
I feel that it, by and large, speaks for itself.
Or I hope it does.
Pee Wee Herman

It was a rare morning, full of anxious secrets, not quite six a.m., with a dying moon on high, birds singing, blue breaking. Martin Worthy was thrilled at mornings, thought of them as enchanted beginnings and got mad that people slept right through them.

A faint glow illuminated his face, a smile that no one was there to see, a smile he felt like smiling only for himself, a sweet and simple vaguely rational pleasure. He was finally accepting the wisdom of a very simple truth. The secret of being uplifted is relaxation. He no longer felt he had to explain himself to anybody, not anybody. No more moral baggage. And it was about time.

It was Martin Worthy's fiftieth birthday. Birthday candles come in boxes of thirty-six and life was an escalating controversy. He found his head a changing universe, a spinning globe, full of a nagging need much of the time; he knew he must get his hands busy. He wanted to get busy but he did not know at what. When he was alone he felt lonely and when he was with the world, the land of slick, he felt empty. Nobody's sure of himself, he thought, the only ones who get along well with that luxury are the ones who enjoy the booming circles of escape; on the contrary, he wanted to fill his space with boundaries.

And six a.m. became nine a.m. and a John Wayne movie was on, *Rio Grande*: 'The Duke plays a tough cavalry commander bent on stopping Indian raids.' He decided that nine a.m. was a fine time for a John Wayne movie because then all the kids could see it. Too bad Elsa was out in Jersey again.

At ten-thirty the mail came. There was a flyer that told him he was 'now able to get a New England masterpiece—the Elijah Stokes table, solid wood with an oak finish for $84.95.' There was a manufacturers' coupon for fifty cents off Ecotrin 'with a safety coating that gives aspirin strength without aspirin stomach upset.' There was a postcard, a 'typical street scene' in Puerto Rico, that was meant for someone named Erinn but was in his mailbox by mistake: Dear Erinn, How ya doin? I'm okay. I'll probably see you before you get this but just wanted you to know I was thinking of you.' And a four page letter from a new health magazine. 'How much do you really know about health and fitness? Answer true or false. Microwaves are low level atomic energy. Severe chest pain is a sure sign of heart disease. Then came some trues. Coffeemate is 65.4% sugar. Elbow and knee replacements are on the way. Hip replacements are already routine. Your heart needs continuous exertion. Stop-and-go exercises like bowling and golf do not serve this purpose.'

He decided he would go to the park and take a book with him. He chose *The Last and Lost Poems of Delmore Schwartz* and opened it at random to page twenty-three and read:

Love and Marilyn Monroe (after Spillane)
Let us be aware of the true dark gods
Acknowledging the cache of the croche
The primitive pure and powerful pink and grey
    primitive sensitivities
Wincing, marvelous in their sweetness, whence
rises
    the future.

It seemed the perfect prop. He closed the cover and, book in tow, set out for the park. In the hallway, picking up his mail, was his young neighbor, always grinning, wide grins, boyish glee.

'How's the baby?' Martin asked. His neighbor was always quick to announce to everyone that his wife had just had a baby who was twenty-one and five-eighths inches long when she was born eighteen days ago with hair the color of carrot juice.

'She's just great,' he said, 'just great.'

Martin stepped outside the hall of the building onto what could loosely be called a stoop but was more like a giant step. His neighbor was all about youth and for a moment he longed for it: youth, dead pan, gracious glibness, gawky high jinks. He was starting to feel his age. No more time for rehearsals. It was this knowledge that wearied him. There could be no more shrieks. He was too reflective for that.

And Martin continued on his way to the park. He wondered whether he was growing old gracefully. He wondered why it still hurt to be alive; do you ever get used to it, being tucked away in an erratic beat, a beat gone sour, yet unique. He liked himself but he was not always sure who else did; this signalled a defect to the owner. He considered his looks: he knew he wasn't sexy.

His looks were passable. There was nothing anyone could point to and call it a mistake.

On the way to the park he passed a sign that read: 'Littering is filthy and selfish so don't do it.' Someone had scratched out the 'don't'. Life was thorough rebellion. A block later he saw some graffiti stretched across a wall: Don't Despair. Just Subvert.

In the park he opened the book to page twenty-three again.

> Therefore, let us praise Miss Marilyn Monroe.
> She has a noble attitude marked by pride and candor
> She takes a noble pride in the female nature and torso
> She articulates her pride with directness and exuberance
> She is honest in her delight in womanhood and manhood
> She is not only a great lady, she is more than a lady,
> She continues the tradition of Dolly Madison and Clara Bow
> When she says, Any woman who claims she does not like
> to be grabbed is a liar . . .
> Whether true or false, this colossal remark
> states a dazzling intention.

Across the park pavement where the pigeons cooed and nibbled over a huge mound of white rice onto which people kept emptying what was left of their lunch, Martin saw a boy lying on his back on a bench with a book propped on his stomach. Alex had a necklace of red and yellow triangles around his neck; they looked like wood but they could have been plastic. The book was *Delmore Schwartz: The Life of an American Poet.* Alex Chase was finishing a book about a new hero and was at the bottom of the page. 'Delmore, who derived such pleasure from the incongruous, would have made much of the bizarre events that followed in the wake of his death.' Martin caught the boy's eye and they smiled, knowing they knew each other from someplace else. Martin walked over. 'Do you like to read poetry as much as you like to write it?'

'It's really songs I write.'

'Well, if you're reading about Delmore Schwartz, you might want to read some of what he wrote.' He handed over the book of poetry to Alex.

On the way home Martin Worthy recalled the free Tuesday evening poetry writing class at St Mark's Poetry Project. The boy had worn glasses then and had straight brown hair. Martin remembered the teacher, a very round man with thin yellow hair who walked in the first night and said, 'Why is everyone sitting in the dark?' and someone answered, 'Because nobody can find the lights.' 'How long is the workshop?' someone had asked. 'Oh, as long as it goes.' The teacher had in his hands a brown paper bag with a can inside which he flipped open. 'Now, as for beer and other addicting stuff, just keep it cool.' After that, the boy always had a bottle of Smirnoff which he kept sipping from all night long on the sneaky path to wisdom.

Later that night Martin Worthy who never drank wandered into a bar where a piano player was playing 'As Time Goes By', and got drunk. He ended up telling a complete stranger, 'I've been blessed with a hell of a lot but my life has never felt full.' He sat there and remembered how when they were kids he and his sister used to bang on metal lampshades with whisk brooms; they wanted to be drummers. He tried to remember the name of one song they used to play over and over again, one of their father's 78 records, something he hadn't heard in years.

He walked out of the bar thinking that old lovers die, old lovers die, and feeling blue because hippie innocence was nothing more than cheap tradition.

The phone was ringing when he got home. 'So how does it feel to be fifty?' his sister wanted to know.

'Safer,' he told her, as though he had the answer ready. 'It feels safer.'

He switched on the television and turned the channels and heard the strains of 'Turkey in the Straw', the song he had been trying to think of all night long, the one that he and his sister used to bang those homemade drums to, the one he hadn't heard for maybe forty years.

The last thing he saw before he went to bed was the television late night news. Authorities identified the body of a twelve-year-old girl who had drowned when she wandered off from an outing with a group called The Aloha High.

And he wished that Elsa was much closer.

CHAPTER FIVE

'Because You Wouldn't Want to Drive Without Your Music'
Clarion Car Audio

On the third Sunday in April Fiarette mailed Alex a birthday card. 'To Alex with love from F.' The front of the card was decorated with multi-colored confetti falling out of the sky on to the Statue of Liberty where a space ship zoomed around the torch. Inside the card was more confetti with a giant sized 'Happy Birthday. Enjoy.' And as she wrote 'with love' she couldn't help thinking that Alex was the kind of person nobody wanted for keeps. She no longer believed that anything that came out of his mouth was true. He lived by the unwritten rules of technical sheen. The last time she had seen him she couldn't wait to get away from the squalor of his room and the soul of his face. Roaches were all over and the food on the stove was dried up and sticking to itself. The priorities of the underprivileged. When they left the room, she on her way and he on his, Alex carried a book and a twig. A twig and a book. An embattled shrine. She knew he was crazy from the look in his eyes but he kissed her as though life was a free cruise instead of a shivering loss. And Fiarette went home and wondered what can you do with people you want to get close to, but not that close.

On Saturday of that same week at two o'clock in the afternoon halfway through the Channel Nine one o'clock movie, *House of Strangers*, with Edward G. Robinson, Susan Hayward and Richard Conte, the telephone rang. Fiarette got mad but she decided to answer it anyway.

'Hello,' Alex said.

'Mmmmm. What's going on?'

'Nothing.'

Silence.

'I was watching a great moving on t.v., eating strawberries and popcorn and I haven't gotten out of my nightgown in two days.'

'What are you depressed about?'

'I'm not depressed. I just feel separated.'

'You didn't even call me on my birthday.'

'Oh, Alex, I sent you a card. You got the card, didn't you? The Statue of Liberty with the space ships flying around it?'

'Yeah.'

'Look, Alex, I really shouldn't have even answered the phone. I'm not into talking.'

'Can I say just one thing?' Alex asked softly.

And Fiarette was thinking how pleasurable it could be to be rude. She also realized this was an essential element for communicating.

'My friend Donna choked on some food and she's in intensive care with brain damage.'

The bearer of glad tidings, Fiarette thought, and stopped the words just in time from coming out of her mouth, searching instead for something vaguely appropriate. She could hear Susan Hayward being downright bitchy to Richard Conte. 'When did it happen, Alex?'

'Two nights ago. She's a real pretty girl, too. She's the

one . . . the guy she was engaged to was murdered on the subway.' His voice cracked and the operator asked for more money.

'Oh, Alex, don't put any more money in. Come on over.'

Alex had no friend Donna. And it wasn't anywhere near his birthday. Alex just never learned to do it right the first time.

Alex had no money. He had tried to work in the plant department of Woolworth's but lasted less than a month. He got bored. The only question anyone ever asked him was how much potting soil was needed to fill an average size window box. The answer was eight pounds.

He knew he was a low grade crazy, fatal but not serious, and spent a lot of hours struggling, a mellow wind picking up speed.

He walked in to Fiarette's apartment and said, 'This guy gave me this book in the park—listen to this great poem about Marilyn Monroe.'

The next morning Fiarette was on the phone with Kary exploring the saga of consolation, the search for balance with no contracts and no memberships.

'We take showers on Saturday morning and never get dried off because we start making love right away while we're still dripping wet. Sometimes it feels like we're never out of each other's touch—we're always stroking backs or holding hands.'

'Sounds good to me, Fee,' Kary said from the telephone in her bedroom to the telephone on Fiarette's kitchen wall.

'Not that good. It's all terribly sensual but Alex wants

to call it love and I don't feel a thing.' Fiarette could hear the coldness in her own voice and reason somewhere in the distance, remote as its name.

And because she knew her friend better than anyone else did, Kary said, 'Oh, Fee, you want to call it love, too. You're just afraid you can't handle it. You want to man the boat.'

'Maybe.' Fiarette opened her refrigerator door, but there was nothing much there. 'Maybe,' she said again. 'Alex likes to play games. He says things like, "I know you like the shy boy look. I could tell the minute I met you that it turned you on." I don't like being second-guessed. He's like an actor checking for effect. Love shouldn't feel like going to a clinic.'

'You just can't see it, Fee. You always want to get away from guys who remind you that you don't like yourself as much as you like to think you do. You always stop being involved the same time round.'

'And I'm getting tired of his silly songs. I'm starting to nag him. It's just not like me.'

'Oh, yes it is. It's just like you. It's just not the way you want to be. That's why it's getting you so upset.'

'Oh, Kary, I don't want to hurt him. He always looks like his heart might stop.' Fiarette felt tears in her eye, the way she always did as a child when she played the part of the elaborate castaway. When she hung up the phone, she felt something surfacing. It was not her; it was someone waiting to be her.

The next morning Fiarette awoke muddy from a night of bad dreams. She decided not to go to work. She didn't go to work for a lot of good reasons. One was that she still didn't understand much more about word processing. She didn't understand anything that had a number in it. The instruction book tried to make it all sound so simple; it told you you could just hit something called a Code 5 to center titles over columns but everything had a trick to it. The whole trauma reminded her of struggling to understand algebra when she was thirteen years old and her math teacher Mother Miriam called her a dullard. The machine, like the heady drama of algebra, made her feel blank. Another reason she didn't want to go to work was that every day she heard the same lines. If it was windy, someone was sure to say, 'I didn't have to take the train, I could have blown in,' or the girl who took off with her makeup case three times a day and always said, 'I'll be in the ladies room to repair the damage.' Elementary monotony with no commercial breaks. She didn't want to go to work because this was National Secretaries Day. There would be a buffet at work in Conference Room 5A and all nonlegal personnel would be invited, and expected, to attend. The coordinator of this graceless hoodwink would come around in the morning and personally hand each secretary, word processor, file clerk and bookkeeper a red carnation with a pearly headed stickpin. Then would come the pale murmured thank-yous. She dialled the office and the girl in Personnel wanted to know, for the record, what was ailing her, but Fiarette didn't know the name. She was heartsick and tired all the time and her favorite outfit was her flannel nightgown. Life was shift and decline two steps to the side, one back, and none ahead. It was nearing early summer but she was always chilled. She thought maybe she might have hepatitis or hypoglycemia or Epstein-Barr syndrome and thought about taking vast amounts of trace minerals and drinking less coffee. She was always angry, ready to do battle, striking out into the future with a mouthful of dirty words.

And so she stayed home on National Secretaries Day

and watched *My Favorite Wife* at one o'clock with Cary Grant and Irene Dunne. At twelve o'clock she had made popcorn for the movie but it was all gone before the movie started.

But she couldn't concentrate on the movie because she kept feeling like everything she touched, she broke.

The sky was fresh in the day but she could not motivate herself to do more than stare at the four walls. Finally she emptied out a Macy's shopping bag that had been sitting on the kitchen floor since last Saturday when she bought pink sneakers in Sportswear and a Silverstone eleven inch frying pan in the Cellar. The final thing to come out of the bag was a flyer:

SOLOMON
WORLD'S GREATEST ASTROLOGER

Tell me your birthday and I will tell you where you've been. I will explain your present and guide you toward your future.
I know all about you.
I can advise you on all areas of your life --
love, marriage, friendship, business and health.
I will take away bad luck and evil influences.
You will bless the day you came to see me.
Consejera y Advinadora

1220 Eighth Avenue
Two flights up

She read it carefully and on this afternoon when life felt like revival in focus she headed for 1220 Eighth Avenue—two flights up.

'You see, dear,' the astrologer was saying, 'you don't

know *how* you should feel.' Her voice was the voice of disposable pop.

Solomon had turned out to be a woman, a very large woman, lavishly confident. 'I have devised my own system for bringing information to you.' Her voice slowed. 'Astrology has so much more to it than just your sun sign. Your rising sign is equally important. And for you, dear, your moon is especially important because your moon is in Cancer. That accounts for your tenacity. Tenacity. The crab is Cancer and Cancer is the crab. You like to hold on to things, especially hurts, old hurts. But the stars are only a guide; we all have free will.'

The astrologer checked the chart again. She wanted to be very sure. The girl had pencilled her time of birth on a small piece of pink memo paper: two thirty-five a.m. Solomon needed that confirmation. It was an unusual aspect in a chart, but there was no doubt what it meant. It meant a loss of identity, something resembling a spell.

'Loss of identity can be a very fruitful experience if other aspects are also present,' she told Fiarette. 'If, for example, it results in positive and unselfish behavior, a person can turn out to be quite a saint.

'Right now, my dear, you are emotionally polarized. Your moon is in the twelfth house, your Pluto, which is power. But in your case that power is like a dumb note. You are too busy in prison with your emotions. I want to put you in touch with certain energy factors. You must have a frame of reference within your realm of flexibility. You keep getting waylaid by something that is only ten minutes away. You must learn to exercise your will. You must use your will to discipline yourself. You are deactivating your will.'

Fiarette felt her dignity being rearranged.

'Now, my dear, you have a very, very good Uranus. Your Uranus is absolutely beautiful. It is trining your Mars. It is trining your Neptune. It is trining your Mercury. And it is trining your sun. Uranus has to do with the will.

'But your moon is in Cancer and you are tenacious and you will not let go. Of what? Of something. Expose yourself and you can expose your weaknesses.

'It is perfectly all right for you to have an identity problem. If your priorities are in order, you will meet the right people. If your priorities are to meet someone who will give you an exciting sex life, that is exactly what you will find. On the other hand, if love and affection are a priority, you can have that, too.

'Remember that confidence means committing yourself to something. You are self-centred in your own reactions and you cannot protect yourself beyond that. It is important for you to be aware of that aspect because what it really means is that you are centered in your own process. And your process is not active but reactive—worrying, wondering, guilt.

'In your past life you must have committed some great sin of lust and passion because those needs are still with you. You are trying to learn to control those passions but you haven't yet succeeded. You like to call it love when it's only lust.'

That night Solomon's words drifted in and out of her consciousness. Fiarette tried to listen, to turn the images into anchors, but she kept losing her place. She examined the notion of identity—what was it? Was it born or made? Was it a private channel, a throbbing fiction? How big a part did she have in creating it, matching it to her needs, maintaining it, this gift-wrapped supple madness? She suddenly realized that time had spots, was a runaway sadness, an untidy pause in her reawakening. Identity was plastic memorabilia, funky but chic.

That night she realized she regretted missing work that day for only one reason: she might have seen David Pond. He worked clear on the other side of the floor and the floor was a long one. But he walked so fast that he was as likely as not to bump into things. She wished he would bump into her.

And somewhere on the other side of town David Pond was tossing away something someone had thrust in his hand one afternoon when he was trying to buy a tie at Macy's. He had been using the flyer as a bookmark but now that the book was finished, he crumbled it and dropped it in the wastebasket. It began,

SOLOMON

CHAPTER SIX

Pilgrim, this is a way of life
Bright as diamonds, cold as ice

Alex Chase's mother was in the kitchen in her Cape Cod style home on Spinning Wheel Drive somewhere in New Jersey. She had just finished reading *My Mother's Keeper* and thought that Bette Davis's only sin was that she had never learned how to be kind enough. She was thinking about her own husband and her married life, the length of eternity. They had just celebrated their twenty-fifth anniversary. Some friends had given a party for the Chases where everyone got frosted glass swans as table souvenirs. Some swans were plain opaque while others had blue points dabbed at their sides that stood for flowers. One still had a price tag stuck to it that said six-ninety-nine. For Mrs Chase time lost some strength at that party; it began to smell serious; it had closing lines.

So she was thinking of her husband, a cruel punch on a magic night. She was wishing she could push him out the window. Every time he blew his nose, he annoyed her. Every time he notched his belt about his thickening waist, he annoyed her. Every time he said, 'Maybe it would look better if I parted it on the other side,' he annoyed the hell out of her. She hid the annoyance from

him and from most everyone else and tried to be sweet
as honey. Their marriage was a dull mistake, which was
the result of a messy romance; he had gotten old so fast,
a surprise collapse, the kind of old where he got tired at
nine o'clock at night. He could feel the murmur of
harmony when his wife was in the same room. He could
see her poised on the balance beam, never seeming to
grow old with him, naive when it came to how much
makeup it was nice to wear. She had insisted on
decorating one corner of their bedroom with her Frank
Sinatra collection. There was a program from the
Westchester Premiere Theater when she had gone up to
New York to see Sinatra one summer night and a poster
from a Carnegie Hall appearance and lots of pictures, 5
x 7's, 8 x 10's, young Frank, older Frank, Frank with
wives, with friends, with children. She was fifty-four
now and she had been a fan for a very long time. She
lived in a land where the lover could be traitor and the
outlaw could be patriot all because of the songs her
favorite singer sang. She felt very close to Frank Sinatra.

The only other picture on her wall was of a smiling
blonde woman, a star of one of the afternoon soaps,
which Alex used to tease her about by calling the show
'The Curious and the Invisible'. Mrs Chase's boyfriend
in New York was the janitor in the building where the
star lived and he got her to autograph it. Her boyfriend,
an Argentinian named Bardinelli, did not comprehend
the marketing tool that was Spinning Wheel Drive. His
world was limited to the fuzzy roar of a few blocks in the
West Village where he worked fixing toilets and firing
up oil burners. And she learned all about making love
through Bardinelli. 'Does sex ever give you the chills?'
she asked her best friend on Spinning Wheel Drive one
day. Her friend had no answer. But because it certainly

sent shivers up and down her spine, as Frank Sinatra might say, Alex's mother really didn't care what it did or didn't do to anyone else.

There was a time when all Alex ever wished from his mother was that they share five husky uninterrupted hours of Monopoly. But now he was a victim of the uneven effects of life's moving parts, art and music.

Alex had thought of sending her a Mother's Day card but after careful consideration decided not to. Most of the cards on Fourteenth Street were in Spanish anyway. He thought about going home if only for Mother's Day itself, but decided against that too. He remembered how last time he went home he had to try not to look at his father, afraid that his own tears would drown him. 'Artists,' his father had said, like a head-on collision, 'let me tell you what I think about artists. Sensitive bums.' Alex did not know what made his father call him an artist. He had never called himself one. Maybe that was a category, a hole where everyone goes who has no place to go, some unsweetened vault. Alex thought of himself as an interpreter of the thick transaction called being here where he had to forestall his own deterioration; he fumbled vaguely with the term 'artistry'. It was a nice excuse to convince himself that reality had nothing to do with him. And he liked the feeling it gave him to write songs.

'Are you close to your father?' Fiarette was asking him. They were at his apartment sorting out his laundry. Fiarette was folding a red fluffy towel and wondering why clothes dryers pull terry apart.

'Close enough.'

'Is that a line I'm supposed to laugh at or a line you'll be using in a song?'

'Let's just say I understand pain and I keep trying to

forget that I understand it so well.' Alex was even more serious than usual, which was very serious indeed. 'As a kid I had a kind of doomed appetite for survival. I felt threatened by too much silence. I felt more comfortable around noise and confusion. I wanted to be everything to everyone. Then I wanted to tell everyone what to do. I wanted them to use my ideas. I wanted to be the whole thing. I fought with everyone, one by one, trying to turn them against one another. And then when there was more chaos than anything else, I was finally satisfied enough to leave.'

'What are you so angry about?'

'It makes me respectable.'

Fiarette could feel herself getting mean. His was a life that was more grin than hunger.

Alex was thinking: his brother Steve, Delmore Schwartz, his mother, the homeless man on Sixth Avenue and Twelfth Street who he finally gave a quarter and two dimes to today, his father. They were all people who moved from day to day, paid bills, told lies, begged for forgiveness, had dreams. They would fall in love and want to kill and change addresses and do it all over again. They would take dance lessons and eat frankfurters and play lotto. And then fade. Someone would go through their pockets and things they saved would be thrown away. And new people would sleep in their beds, open their windows, paint their bathrooms, lock their doors. A lifetime seemed suddenly so short to him; he could see a year swallowed up by a decade and then by a generation.

Alex clasped his hands behind his head and said, 'I think I'll write a song about my brother Steve.

He's a lady
name of passion
and he drives a Chevy van.
He's playing double agent all the time.

He stopped the imaginary guitar in mid-air and said, 'All we are is people in each other's lives, people going on.'

Fiarette looked at him sitting on the window sill, perched, one leg up to his chest, the other one too close to the window ledge. He had been wearing the same white t-shirt for weeks now.

Off the ledge and into the refrigerator to take out a big chunk of watermelon. 'I got this whole piece for fifty-eight cents,' Alex announced. 'It was only twelve cents a pound at Key Food; the Korean store is selling it for twenty-five cents a pound.' Alex sat down at the table and one by one removed the seeds from the red watermelon. 'Watermelon is a respectable sweet.'

They stayed together for hours and hours until it was late on an early summer night that would soon turn into morning and they were on the street to get away from the sticky heat of Alex's room. Alex lay on the hood of a car and Fiarette bent over next to him. The street lights made him look freewheeling but reverent and his black eyes glowed. He clasped his hands behind his head and studied the orange moon.

A voice hit the night. 'Joyce, you bitch, give me back my property.'

'What's that?' Fiarette wanted to know.

'Interesting story.'

Joyyyyyyyyyyyyyccccce.'

'He's drunk,' Alex said. 'I've seen them together when he's sober and they look so happy. He was in the hospital last year, almost died, but when he came home he was right back on the bottle. He hollers for her all the time.'

'Joyce, give me my property.' The guy yelled up at a window.

'What does he mean by property?'

'His bottle, probably.'

'Joyyyyyyyyyce.'

Something came flying out the window.

'And my cane,' he yelled up. 'Give me my cane.'

'Here comes the cane,' said Alex, as something else came flying out. All was quiet then as they heard him shuffling towards the car and past it, cane and crutches.

'See, that's what he meant by his property,' Alex said. 'She loves him but she doesn't want to. Any woman who takes care of a man like that has to love him.'

And the next night Alex had called Fiarette at one o'clock in the morning. 'Are you busy?'

'Busy? At one o'clock in the morning?'

"Well, can I stop by for a cigarette.'

'You're good for my head,' he told her when he got there. 'I know I'm always doing all the talking but you're the only one I know who lets me do that.'

'That's all right, Alex.' She was trying to be patient, but she felt herself squirm. 'I'd rather talk about you— this way I can leave myself out of it. I keep telling you I'm a loner. As much of life as I can do alone I want to do alone. There's very little I can't do by myself. I can take walks alone, eat alone, swim alone, dance alone, think alone. I don't even need people to talk to.' She could feel her teeth.

'How do you survive?' he said in simple honest amazement.

'It's a lot better than that. I feel safe. I feel safe just staying away from people. It's a wall, but it's a happy wall. Do you think that sounds crazy? Or just selfish?'

'I don't know,' Alex said. 'I'll have to think about it for a while.'

'Maybe that's the trouble, Alex. You have to think about it. Maybe you don't protect yourself enough. Being with another person is always a risk. You have to be armed. Just remember that no one starts out to inflict pain; it's a by-product of being fragile, of people's contrary natures. The crowded heart. You have to learn how to stay with yourself.'

And later that morning when the orange moon was nowhere to be found, Alex sat at his kitchen table and picked up some yellow sheets of paper on which he had scratched song lyrics.

> There were things he always felt
> but he didn't know their name.

He changed this to:

> There were things he always felt
> but they didn't have a name.

And added:

> But he would have paid attention all the same.

He turned to another sheet:

> I'm getting ready for the night to end
> When I'll end up alone.

He scrapped that one, a tight wad of paper against the wall. It had been a long time since he had actually

finished a song. Alex went to sleep that night thinking
that his life was no longer a lot of problems; it was more
like a series of moods. He dreamed he was flying and
seemed able to stay aloft by pushing downward on the
currents of air much as a swimmer paddles down water.

The day after Mother's Day Martin found himself eating
a tuna fish sandwich and looking over some booklets he
had picked up summers ago. He remembered going in
the building on Fifth Avenue with the Atlas out front
and down the escalator to the New England Vacation
Center. Along the wall were folders and maps and
brochures for every New England state. Connecticut,
Massachusetts, Rhode Island, New Hampshire, Vermont
and Maine. He headed for the section on Maine and took
maps and flyers and booklets, as many as he could
without feeling guilty. Now he was studying one of them:
Maine Guide to Fishing. The cover was of a man with
high rubber boots, knee deep, fly casting. Once he had
cast a line like that, back when he was eleven or twelve
years old. His father had taken him fishing because his
older brother wasn't interested in going. He wasn't that
interested himself, but he went because he wanted his
father's attention. He remembered his father standing
behind him, holding his wrists and showing him how to
fly cast. He remembered the moment, only the moment.
    Now he looked at the ad and wished his father was
still around to share it with: '. . . promises bass, trout,
salmon, perch and pickerel, on a twelve mile pond.'
There were ads for fishing camps with names like
Whisperwood and Whipporwill and Cozy Cove in
places like Lake Pennesseewasee. He didn't know what
to do with the booklet; he couldn't just throw it away.

From his father his thoughts went to his mother. Her favorite expression of anger had been 'Damn it to hell.' He remembered that film *Far From the Madding Crowd* and how he had been discussing it with his mother because Otto Preminger, the director, had been on one of those afternoon talk shows and she had seen him.

'Otto Preminger was on television today talking about *Far From the Madding Crowd*.'

'It's maddening, mom,' he had insisted in crisp finality.

'I'm sure it's madding,' she had said.

'It's not; there's no such word.'

She had been too wise to argue with someone as stubborn and righteous as he. But later that night she left the newspaper open to the ad for *Far From the Madding Crowd*. He never said a thing, never admitted he was wrong, and now he understood suffering, the deficiency of being unkind, when you are alone and life duplicates the pain.

CHAPTER SEVEN

Purity is a distraction
after you reach eleven

The white rose was the last one to open up. Fiarette
looked at it there in the vase in her kitchen and was
reminded that budding is what makes things beautiful.
You have to let it happen, the sense of taste. Alex had
brought her three roses, one white, one yellow, one red.
She had gone through the motions of acting as though
she was excited by them, carefully, attentively, lovingly
snipping the stems and placing them one by one in a
vase of water, neither too warm nor too cold. All the time
she was thinking in morbid poignancy that for three
lousy bucks, a buck a rose, no one was going to play
cheap tricks on her. She wouldn't allow it. That was
Thursday night. Now it was Saturday and the white rose
was the last to open. Alex had come and gone, a life
scarcely out of shadow, and she knew he was someone
she was not meant to love; she knew the symptoms of
resistance, the ageless chic of needing your own space.

They argued about crazy stuff like what row to sit in
at a movie. He wasn't happy unless he sat in the first five
rows. His arms were never a circle around her; they were
closer to a grip. She realized she would rather fantasize
about David Pond. So she walked over to her bed and

lay there on her back staring into the apricot and yellow flowers on her wallpaper, fingering the insides of her bra, lost on a dirt road. Her hand slipped in a tiny bit more and thought of David Pond and what it would be like with his hand where hers was right now. She was a grinning rocket.

That was when she decided she would go to Macy's on Saturday and get some super sheer stockings for work and then go downtown and buy an extra half ounce purse-size bottle of Ambergris perfume oil so she could have it with her at all times. She wanted David Pond to smell her. She wanted them to pick up the boundaries of each other's scents, close in, drink Pina Coladas, ignite the nourishment and make unlimited love.

And she decided more. She would never ever have another piece of cotton underwear in her wardrobe, no matter how well cotton breathed. No stretched out elastic on anything, no lacy hems ready to come down. From now on all her underthings would be silk or at least feel like it, colored late spring, faint blues the color of flowers, late night pinks, yellows the colors of sunsets on buildings in New York afternoons. She wanted David Pond to look at her and be tempted; she wanted him to think what a delightful romance great sex can be. She wanted him to know what was on her mind.

Everywhere else in her life there was no life. Her dreams were her balloons.

She found no delight in Alex; he blocked her spirit with his squalor. He always matched his socks and shorts and, no matter how heated the passion, always took the time to slip his shorts off so they stayed right side up as they came off his legs and over his shoes. Last to come off was always the shoes. Alex was one of those things that lasts a long time without ever achieving the status of a romance.

Sex is important only when it's great. Otherwise, it's an inconvenience. If it doesn't make you high as a mountain, why bother? If it's too tentative, who needs it? And with Alex sex had become something to do, like eating junk food. It passed the time, wiped up the excess passion, and hid the twisting and groaning emotions. It was as easy as shaking hands and that made it too easy. She was after untamed pounding.

She wondered what kept them together. Their bond rested on a history of untruths. The ones that seemed necessary at the beginning and the ones that then seemed essential until the entire relationship was refreshed by superlatives. They were lies that neither punctured nor ruptured, but their persistence made them poisonous. Feelings became a measure of control, a sparring of egos, and Fiarette knew she could go on winning as long as she chose to go on playing. But she wanted to be loyal to her training manual and knew it was time to move on.

She was a concept to Alex, a fledgling shelter, flat survival, someone who had the patience for his anxieties. Her patience was exhausting her.

She had to end it. She panicked now at the state of her feelings. Two weeks ago she had almost told Alex she loved him. Then she was seized with this notion that he had outsmarted her into feeling this and she had let go.

But she was still inclined to spend ninety cents on a card that said 'You're the best thing that ever happened to me.' It was something she wanted to say to somebody so she said it to him. She wanted to be part of someone's emotions; otherwise there was too much blue in the room. Alex's card came in a paper bag full of lyrical script that said 'Caring is the art of sharing.' The bag with the card stayed on the oak washstand in her dining room until one day prompted by a spark of love she dropped a stamp on it and ran out to a mailbox. The blue eased up in the room.

Then Alex got a job at Sak's Fifth Avenue doing maintenance work. Every single morning he had to be there at six a.m. to vacuum the entire third floor. She was sorry she had sent the card. She, who was so afraid of heights, wanted to climb a mountain. She no longer wanted to wrestle with truth and the routine of daily remodeling. She didn't know who was doing the lying, but the accuracy of love just wasn't there. It was one more blind corner, the way you know you'll never get to go to any real good parties after you hit forty.

Now every time she thought of Alex she made a sour face. If something was real, all he wanted to do was write a song about it.

'People who consider themselves lucky usually are losers,' he had told Fiarette. 'The smell stays put.'

And she had answered, 'Don't spill water on the table,' because as usual Alex wasn't watching where he put his glass.

'Don't worry about it. Life is no fun when you have to start worrying about what happens to the things you own.' He thought she wasn't listening to him, but she was, more than ever, like echoes that take too long to get lost.

Her thoughts about Alex were scanty. And there was a delicate gloom in her eyes that could almost pass for mischief.

Work was making her want to explode. Her boss had just returned from flying home to a hospital in California to see her mother who had just had a stroke. On the plane she had ripped her last pair of panty hose and panicked, knowing her mother would demand, as always, that she look perfect. Then she remembered she was going to see someone who had been in a coma for nineteen hours. When her boss came back, Fiarette asked how the mother was doing; 'unsalvageable,' was the answer: a prognosis for a recyclable. Her boss was at a point in her life where her everyday life style was being adopted from magazines like *Computer News Now*.

Work was a monster. Every morning just after coffee break, the company's daily bulletin came around. Over blueberry muffins and buttered sesame bagels everyone waited for *The Daily News* which everyone called *The Daily Snooze*.

This morning Fiarette sat at her desk trying to make sense out of this: 'The columnar date $\frac{1}{2}$ has been placed outside the column. Because the display shows the code backspace, the $\frac{1}{2}$ will appear further to the right on the screen than on the printout.' There was one thing about work that she liked: it was a place where there were rules. Her identity was more and more the faded rose, and she cherished discipline and direction. She had never been one to find out what happened to someone who broke rules. She broke only the ones that nobody could possibly know about and those were the ones she made up herself. This way she maintained her innocence.

That night one of the discos in midtown was having a search for Face of The Year. Cissy was telling everyone how she had bought her tickets weeks before (fifteen dollars in advance, twenty at the door). 'I'm going right home after work to get ready,' she said, airing her plastic black and white bangles and her plastic drop earrings. 'I'm going to splurge and take the express bus.' Cissy was a tall skinny blonde who took half a lude and couldn't understand why she felt dizzy. She was in need of a few more traffic lights. A month before the doctor had discovered a small but benign tumor and she rushed right out and bought Bal à Versailles perfume. Someone once said to her: 'I'll bring the intelligence; you bring the wine.' But she didn't get it.

Work was slow and they sat there with nothing to do. Ronnie was tossing out names for the baby she would have soon. In the Jewish tradition he or she had to be named after two deceased people, an aunt and an uncle, the first an 'A' name and the second a 'C' name. Ashley Celeste, Avery Chad, Adam Charles, Allison Ceil. Someone else was clipping out tummy exercises from *Cosmopolitan* and xeroxing them. Everyone was bored and getting into minor food fantasies: Cissy wanted vodka and cranberry juice; Ronnie wanted M and M's— 'the box, not the bag.' Fiarette was thinking, if there's no work why can't we just go home?

The next day she told herself relaxation meant not being afraid of yourself no matter what. So she went to lunch alone and found that the closer you get to anything, the grainier it becomes. She felt the spiral of lapsing into solemnity. She was feeling less and less comfortable. In the park a breeze blew the scent of flowers her way. She was thinking that the longer David Pond knew her or knew of her, the harder it would be, the less likely it would be, that he would go to bed with her.

She was getting angrier and angrier with each passing day; she would not permit herself to laugh life off. By not getting angry she knew she would be forfeiting her feelings. But she was angry at too many things for a steady focus. One night she understood that her parents never knew what it was that they didn't like about themselves. She had watched them fail at everything they tried, needs so shallow they had yet to earn the respectability of being called a dream. They died because they had no nerve.

Nothing much happened to Fiarette the day after that. She broke a fingernail, decided she didn't like the way the skin of a papaya tasted, and realized it would be another summer of soccer and reggae in Washington Square Park. Alex would never accept that she didn't need him and would go through life with his hand out. She ate an apple when what she really wanted was a Milky Way.

Outside the early evening rain was light but steady. It quieted the city down. It made her sad and finally it made her sob. Fiarette remembered what many of us remember on a rainy day: the best refuge is sobering sleep. She felt the risk of always needing to do things her way. She was more determined than ever that no one notice she was made of glass. She felt she was making mistakes more often than she should for a full stage dress rehearsal. She was not interested in being human in a world of corroded patterns; she longed for super human. Yet she was too weak even to sustain a relationship; it absorbed more of her than was even there. Dead in her head, Fiarette stopped the words and let the feeling of loss take over. She would never be mature enough to be happy. She would always be in need. She would always be in pain.

She rubbed Mill Creek aloe vera moisturing cream on her right leg clear up her thigh and Nivea skin oil on her left one. Which one smelled better? Would they smell the same to David Pond as they did to her? The Mill Creek was orangey and the Nivea just creamy. She wasn't sure. She knew she better decide on just one. She didn't want to smell one way one time and another way the next.

She ate a whole pound of red grapes, nibble by nibble, slept, got up to watch *Malibu Beach* on television, and found it was getting harder and harder to be nice to Alex. It felt rough growing old. Youth is all around you, on t.v., off t.v. She nursed a fever blister with Blistex. You either find someone with a hook and ladder or you learn how to take care of yourself.

How much of this am I supposed to comprehend? she asked herself. How much of this do you want to comprehend? another part of her responded. And went on: Let me put it to you gently. You must decide whether you wish to understand or to be understood. Few people are able to manage both. The voice was strong and patient and she knew it was on her side. Do I have to decide right now? she pleaded. The sooner you decide, the less time you'll waste going over it again and again.

CHAPTER EIGHT

Collecting God

Martin was at his friends' house somewhere in south Jersey where they were hoping for the rain to come and give their lawn a good soaking. They wondered aloud if maybe they should turn on the garden hose and let it sprinkle the ground for a while until the rains came. One of the women, in a turquoise dress with a hand-crocheted collar, was talking about a special raspberry syrup that she liked to put at the bottom of a glass of beer. Then she talked about a metal cat she had picked up at a barn auction that she was using as a doorstop. He watched his host point out the poison ivy patch to the gardeners, a black couple, man and wife; the man had no teeth although he couldn't have been more than forty. Someone was saying that the three most important qualities in a friend are being sincere, being communicative, and being interesting.

'In that order?' he was asked.

'Not necessarily.'

Martin was thinking about consumerism, the addiction to buying things. Little boxes become bigger boxes and shoe boxes become closets; flimsy containers are replaced by cardboard ones, strong enough to be able to

house the have-ables safely and forever. Getting and
spending were American rights, American trinkets,
good to the last drop. The pain is lifted from living
amidst hurrahs of let's get to bed and let go. And one is
allowed the indulgence of considering it urgent that the
color of shelf lining paper match a stripe in a kitchen
towel. All I wanted to do all summer was swim, he was
thinking. The water, the smell of the water, the
wonderful way water smells, being in the water, near the
water, there is time to think in the water. I never got a
chance to swim this summer. The few days I got to the
beach the ocean was so cold. I never got to a pool, never
saw a lake. I still keep smelling water. Those were his
thoughts while he lay back on the yellow and white
chaise on the deck of his friends' home, a deck of Jersey
cedar, the kind that silvered while the breeze made
shapes. The deck looked out over the marshes, protected
by the Wetlands Act; later on when fall turned to winter
ducks and geese would fly over the house, sometimes a
hundred geese at a time, honking hungrily. 'Then you
know it's going to get cold,' his friends had told him.
'They wake you up in the middle of the night,' his
friend's wife said. 'I always get out of bed and come up
and look. They honk and honk and honk.' A gaggle of
geese, Martin was thinking, a flock of birds, a school of
fish, a warren of rabbits. He wondered if this migration
of geese happened only at night like Santa Claus.

And so went his thoughts on that afternoon.

Someone talked about an article he had read in the
Times magazine about how you have to wait fifteen
years for an apartment in Poland and seven for a
telephone.

The telephone shook the room. Martin's thoughts
were somewhere around the maldistribution of power.

And then the voice. 'You'd better sit down. I have some bad news, Martin.'

'Who?' The answer was Elsa.

Elsa was dead. The morning newspaper would carry a few short paragraphs about it. A young girl with a strong interest in chemistry was fatally injured experimenting with explosives in the apartment she lived in with her father. It was not, the newspaper continued, a radical act; no pipe bombs were found.

Sanity being slower and more deadly than insanity, the days passed.

Elsa was dead. He felt anger but he didn't know where. He understood with a shock the permanence of passion: you never stop loving someone you have truly loved, no matter how it turns out.

Death, a code word. People's sympathies floated in on cards and letters, sentiments from friends sharing their losses so your loss might be lightened. But it never worked: no death is like any other and everyone must understand it in his own way.

In his head he heard the words to 'Beautiful Dreamer'; the voice was so clear. Was it a record of his father's he was recalling? 'Beautiful dreamer, queen of my song.'

Elsa: head-on visions of pivotal moments. She got such a kick when he let her blow out a match after he lit a cigarette. In the wondrous way children do, she could express her joy at the moment; when something great happened, she cheered, loudly, right on the spot. She knew she was having a good time while it was still going on. He could see her now in the green and white ruffled dress he thought was too long but she thought was just right. He remembered the night she had let the dog jump up on her lap while she was still at the kitchen table; the dog ate the hamburger on her plate and he had punished her by making her go without dinner. He could hear her telling the story about the 'lady on the bus who kept going "sh, sh, shushhhh"'; she would tell him the story again and again, especially the "sh, sh, shushhhh" part until he had wanted to choke her.

His mourning became a mixture of sorrow and remorse. He wished he had been kinder, to Elsa, to everyone. He knew he had always let himself come first; his love was worthless because he wasn't mature enough to let it be of any use.

He thought of the ways they had been alike, a fifty-year-old man and his eleven-year-old daughter: there had been many. He was grateful she had never learned to hate.

Death, waking up with it, grief that absorbs all and gives back nothing. He tried to deny his sadness but every minute was difficult, conspicuous; he felt the terrible force of anguish; he was blocked, diminished, humiliated. He sobbed but sometimes did not have energy enough even for that. He wanted to fight, to pummel, to pound, but simply endured. He slept twelve hour days and had no one, nor wanted anyone, to discuss death with. He longed to feel pleasure, to understand triumph, however slight. But nothing reached him and he would never, he was sure, love another thing.

Martin Worthy sat in the bathtub, the water hotter than usual, turned on hard, coming at him from the shower nozzle high above. He felt it lashing him and that was the way he liked it. He let it slap on his neck while he put his chin to his chest and, looking down, counted the spiral openings in the metal drain—one, two, three . . . nine, ten, eleven, and then two, four, six. A

Bandaid was floating towards the drain. And two washcloths, a navy one and a pink one. Why do I have two washcloths when I am only one person? And then he became concerned that the shower was taking too long and he was wasting water. He wanted to stay put in that state of daze but he made himself get out. He realized he really did not want to waste water and got furious because he knew that would never occur to most people. He wondered why he was always burdened by believing he was taking more than his share; tonight it was water, tomorrow it could be hope. And yet he never honestly felt he had enough. He was always wanting. And he was angry at being alone. His growing restlessness demanded him to be with someone all the time now but he knew it was isolation he must reckon with. And whoever dallied with him soon learned to let him have his own way; he wanted now to control, to say goodbye first, to be at the head of every table, and at no one's mercy. I do not want to be left alone. Don't die on me. Please.

A sad mask was taking over his face, the same face that up until now he had been so sure never would change. He began spending too much time after that looking at his face in extreme close up in his mirror. He did not know what he was looking for, some small hint of motion. It was what he had been that concerned him; he had been young in the days of girls and the chaos of martinis.

He could not remember when he had last changed the sheets on his bed. The sheets unchanged and lived in soon gave the bedroom the smell of dirty socks. Dear God, he prayed, why have you left me behind?

Elsa was gone but Elsa was everywhere. Who would she have grown up to become? How deep were her thoughts?

What were her questions? What would her questions have come to be? Her reality had been so distinct.

He found a note sent to him and his wife when Elsa had been born. It had a baby in a pink bonnet with a pink bow on a pink background with white polka dots. Inside it said:

> It wasn't easy
> To know what to choose.
> But hope this is something
> that baby can use. Love, John and Pat

He didn't remember who they were.

He found Elsa's ink blot paintings. One was of animals dancing in the rain. Another looked like a pink fish. He found pages from a coloring book she had when she was much younger: a horse with a yellow hat and an orange tail on a page with a capital H next to a small h in the upper left hand corner. On the capital E small e page was an elephant and a man riding him balancing an egg on one finger. That page wasn't colored in yet, but he knew she would have enjoyed it; it had lots of stripes.

He came across her *Alice in Wonderland* book; the front cover was coming off. He wanted to save that cover. It had pictures of everyone on there: the Gryphon, Alice herself, holding a pig in her arms and the rabbit with a coat of many hearts. He began to read: 'In another moment down went Alice after it, never once considering how in the world she was to get out again . . . Either the well was very deep, or she fell very slowly, for she had plenty of time as she went down to look about her, and to wonder what was going to happen next. First, she tried to look down and make out what she was coming to, but it was too dark to see anything . . . Down, down,

down. Would the fall *never* come to an end? "I wonder
how many miles I've fallen by this time? I must be
getting somewhere near the centre of the earth. Let me
see: that would be four thousand miles down, I think." '

He closed the book. Elsa was at the centre of the earth.
The thought frightened him. It could happen to anyone.

And the headline on the back of the *New York Post* was
Mets Bop Sox.

CHAPTER NINE

Being With You
Is Like Being at an Intersection

Fiarette and Kary were sitting in Burger King beneath an orange sign with yellow letters, 'Home of the Whopper.' Fiarette was thinking about lunch last week with Cissy, that tall skinny blonde at work, and how she sat there chewing carrots for lunch and being satisfied. And here, she, Fiarette, the pig, was about to order a double cheeseburger and large fries, and maybe a vanilla milkshake. The girl next to them had a face like Diana Ross and was with a man who was conning her into thinking what a good idea it would be if he moved in with her. His hand slid up and down her leg.

'Do you think popcorn could pop inside you?'

Fiarette looked at Kary.

'I mean, if there's a kernel that hasn't popped yet, but it's just about to . . .'

'No more, please, Kary. I wouldn't worry about it.'

'I'm not worried about it. I was just wondering.'

'Don't eat them if you're going to think about that; don't eat the ones that haven't popped, okay?'

'But I like the way they taste.'

'And stop being cute.'

Fiarette sat across from Kary, tiring of her, bored with

her, two kids celebrating their egos. While Kary continued to convince herself of the need for monstrous stretches of lazy moonlight, she herself felt damned; she longed for the natural healing of being a hermit. She could hear herself say it. 'I want to be a hermit.'

'Where would you like to be a hermit?'

'Goa.'

'What are you looking for, Fee?' Kary knew when her friend needed a cue.

'Signposts.' She wanted to be talked out of her anger. She was feeling much too mean. She wanted to hurt Kary but she wanted Kary to escape. 'Signposts,' she said again. 'I feel so disconnected at times. I look up at the sky and it crumbles me.'

'Me,' Kary said, 'I just want to be amused.'

'Bad habits are a way of delaying real life, Kary.' Her voice was patience in prison.

'Why do you keep junking my head, Fee?' Her voice quaked.

'Your life is like rush hour. You want me to hand you the anesthetic. You think you're good at making decisions but you're not. You quit jobs at the wrong times. You fall in love with the wrong people. You fall out of love with the right ones.'

'There never are any right ones.'

'I wonder why.' Fiarette glared at her friend. 'Maybe you're just having too much fun. It's hard to have a lover when what you really want is half a block of men running after you.'

Out on the street they saw a man choke, maybe to death, just beyond the revolving doors of a store on Sixth Avenue that sold futons. A man was bending over the victim and putting a small flashlight near his tongue. The victim's body gave a huge heave. Kary and Fiarette, united in fear, kept right on walking once they found out what was going on. They felt the loud hum of death.

'Did I ever tell you how sometimes I think I could be happy in prison?' Kary said. 'I like the idea of being forced to stay in such a sad place where other people make your rules for you. You wouldn't have to waste time wondering what to do next or if you spent too much time on the wrong things.'

Fiarette was paying attention only to herself. She felt like fighting. When I get mad, I get sick. The words came very slow, very certain inside her head. When I get sick, I get mad. The next thing she heard was Kary finishing a story. '. . . and out of everybody in the room, he wanted me.' Fiarette did not know if Kary was relating something that had already happened or if it was the way Kary wished it could be; Kary was always bouncing between now and more to come.

'You just want to be more important than you are, Kary. You never really define yourself.' Over the whelping of a dog and the high cut of a siren curving a corner. 'Empty your pockets out, start from scratch, stop being one of the misinformed.' She wondered if she meant misinformed or uninformed; she decided it was misinformed.

After they parted, Kary rounded a corner close to home and saw Margie, the old woman in the neighborhood.

'I'm having trouble with my eyes these days,' she told her. 'And I think of how my own good mother grew old and her eyesight began failing. She always blamed it on the light. She'd look up at the lightbulb and shake her head. You need a lot of patience growing old.

'You have a lot of boyfriends, don't you?' she said to the girl, but Kary never answered her. She forced a smile and walked faster. She was afraid of old women. 'You have emotions that haven't happened yet,' the old woman said. Her call was prophetic and made Kary panic.

When she was home and alone she said, 'Let the whole world go to pot,' and, laughing, took another toke.

CHAPTER TEN

From the *Sunday Times* Real Estate Section:
Is There a Doctor in Manhattan
Who doesn't secretly yearn for an office on Central Park?

Martin woke up the next morning thinking of her, his wife, how fifteen years ago they had lived in that little apartment in the Village, two rooms and half, whose redeeming feature if you cranked your head wide to the right was a fractional view of the Empire State Building. He remembered one day even more than fifteen years ago when they had woken up to the rain and decided they would play hookey from work and go to the movies. It was a Friday, an all-day rain. He remembered the movie was *Zabriskie Point*.

At night he put on the water for coffee and the radio for company. He listened to the weather or the latest news about a baseball strike. On Sundays he might go to his sister's; one afternoon she asked him to nail down some loose floor boards on her white wooden wrap-around porch. He remembered how Elsa used to watch him work, how she would sit on the edge of the hammock, her hands in her little lap. He felt the anger, awful and untamed, and banged the nails hard into the floorboards.

When the anger let up, the loneliness took over. But he didn't know what to do with it. Sex had started to feel like something only other people do. He felt that his days with women were over. He seemed to meet only women who didn't know what the *New York Times Book Review* was. Yet sometimes they were preferable to the complicated types who didn't like him because he wasn't quite complicated enough. He would think lines like 'I don't drink, but I want a drink,' while she said 'I used to be a married woman; now I'm just a single tramp' and expect him to laugh. And at some point he would tell himself he was a snob when it came to making love to a woman, and he wondered if that made him more or less of a man. And every little maneuver with someone of the opposite sex lacked deliciousness and more and more he wanted to be alone. Sex was an abbreviation. Sometimes he would want women to beg him to spend the night together, but he knew that was ego. He really didn't want to have to fuss with anything in the mornings except himself. Even when he was young, love was something to attach time to, coping in space, the humor of getting by, moving in another direction, physics. That realization spilled over Martin after a lazy midday nap, the kind of sleep that takes you by surprise and knocks you out cold. No one bothered to ask why he seemed more and more content to stay quietly at home. He never planned it. It just happened. That midday Martin was in bed at home with a paperback he had picked up at a flea market on Canal Street. 'She brought out the bottle and we drank slowly.'

Norman Mailer's words made him drift, awakened in him a torrid romance with the clang and grit of words. Writing. Words together. He hadn't written since college; he went for only a semester before he had to leave to get a job. But he remembered how much he had enjoyed writing. 'Write simply,' his teacher had admonished.

'Don't write a word until you know it like an old shoe.
Read *A Farewell to Arms*, Hemingway, and note the
precision and simplicity.'

Later his teacher had told him. 'A writer has it over
the painter, the film maker, the sculptor. He can suggest
inward states of feelings and thought more completely
because he can more completely reproduce living
experience.'

141–F—that was the course number that college
semester where he labored over his papers, papers that
came back from the teacher with notes in red like
'Tighter,' 'a bit confusing,' 'colloq. – avoid,' and the
occasional 'good usage.' Papers like 'Was King Oedipus
Pre-Destined?' or a critique on Katherine Mansfield's
The Garden Party or Wilbur Daniel Steel's *How
Beautiful with Shoes*.

In red: 'Don't mess around with your subjective
feelings—you have a craft to learn.'

He left school, started working, got married and never
thought about writing again. Until now. He did not
know where it came from, this desire to write, this
command to thrust and enter. He rolled a sheet of typing
paper into his old portable and filled it with thoughts
running fast, and once all the typing was done for the
day, he numbered the pages in red pencil. What he
wrote seemed to come from nowhere, to be recorded at
pre-set speeds, programmed with no obvious relevance
to before or after. He was grateful for the writing and
understood that it hid the anger; it controlled the gap.

And on nights when he would wake up with a thick-
ness in his throat and tears in his eyes he would
remember he was a writer and so he would write. At four
o'clock in the morning he would hunt and peck for what
would come next. He realized with a bang how

desperately he wanted to be good at it, this journey that changed feelings into words. And the next day and the day after that he would lie across his bed after dinner and hear lines being written inside him, characters set against luxuriant backdrops, or stuck on humble steps. He saw them and they became real. He did not know where they came from, but only that he could give them life, make them immaculate voices or shoot them down along the way. It was all up to him, but he felt the strange sorrow of needing to do it right.

He wondered if growing up meant no longer apologizing for yourself, finally having no one to answer to. He considered getting a new typewriter and maybe even a new desk chair. Then he decided that the old Smith Corona was a hell of a fast keyboard and maybe a new ribbon was all he needed. He remembered studying about the effortlessness of great fiction. And as he wrote he thought of Norman Mailer's words in *An American Dream*: 'I could feel my heart beating now like a canary held in my hand.'

Days later he found a note he had written to himself:

1. Glue bottom of tool box.
2. Glue piece on bathroom vanity.
3. Can I write a good story?
4. Eagle pens.

And suddenly, more than ever, he was writing. It wasn't easy. It wasn't ever easy. 'People don't want to write, they want to "have written"'. He placed these words of Graham Greene above his typewriter. Yet, difficult, treacherous, as it was, he felt centered only when he was writing. It both lifted him and reminded him that life is learning how to take the punishment. He began to think of himself as a writer and knew that writing was more than just words. His emotions were those of a writer, stalked constantly by an intensity that demanded the written word. Writing pulled him to shore and slowly he could feel structure coming into his work.

His writing had the taste of home made. It felt right. The act of writing put him at ease, stopped the flow of fierce impatience. Conversations bored him. He tried to listen but that was worse than talking and he began to feel that because he was a writer it would be perfectly acceptable to stop talking. Whatever it took to get him to stop running and to sit down was okay. It was what he was meant to do and he allowed himself to believe not another thing mattered.

He told a friend that writing gave him tangible evidence of what he did with his emotions in the course of a day. The assassin and the apprenticeship. It was something he was good at, this putting people together. Sometimes he knew he wanted only to hide and was grateful that he had found an honorable way of doing it.

But today the only thing he could come up with in four hours of writing was the name of a character for a book or a short story. He wasn't sure which. He was full of possibilities and postponed the writing by going out to buy mushrooms and spinach and picking up a newspaper with a cover story about a mother who drowned four of her children. He looked at the movie section and noticed that two movies were playing: *I Married a Shadow* and *The Man Who Wasn't There*. He chuckled and turned the page.

CHAPTER ELEVEN

.

Fringe Benefits Are The Benefits
Of Living On The Fringe

Alex stood there fingering the glossy pages of the latest
issues of all his favorite magazines. He felt like wasting
time and wondered how long he could stand there in the
candy store skimming all the magazines he wanted
before the Arab who owned it did something more than
just stare wildly at him.

Out on the street he passed the old lady Margie. Alex
gave her dog a cold french fry and the dog ate it and
licked his lips. The woman smiled and said, 'That dog is
my psychological nightlight.' She was sitting on a stoop
writing in a black and white notebook.

'What's that?' he asked.

'My book of wishes,' Margie answered.

'What's in it?'

'A teal blue dress with shoes to match.'

Alex was always high these days and walked around
with a clipboard that he had picked up on Canal Street;
he liked people to think he was capable of making
urgent observations; he liked people to think he was
carrying a weapon.

On Sunday Alex was going to visit his parents and his
mother had asked him to pick up some baklava at

Poseidon Bakery on the west side of Ninth Avenue. Sometimes his mother made him feel like a delivery boy. She always wanted something that she claimed could be found only in New York City. He wondered where she found out about these things if they could be found only in New York City.

In the stationery store he studied a poster. It was of two women exactly alike diving like arrows into an ice blue swimming pool. Behind them was a row of palm trees, each one exactly alike, each one blowing in the same breeze. In the foreground were two poolside umbrellas, each one exactly alike. It was about repetition, the sad domesticity of continuity, staring at prison walls, crossing off days.

He wondered how sexual relationships became unsexual ones. He could feel it happening with Fiarette. It was change, a brief dark shadow and it made him shiver. It scared him how bad things can happen to you and you have a feeling it's going to get worse even though you've never been there before. It made him feel like he had been staying in the wrong town for too long but the next bus was a week away.

Alex was feeling poor today. He was saving his money for the bus fare for Sunday when he would go home to New Jersey. He had to make a choice right now between taking the subway three or so miles home or buying two pounds of nectarines on the street for a dollar. He decided on the nectarines, ate three right away, and pretty much didn't mind the walk home. He was thinking about writing a song called 'Give up your day job.'

By Sunday night he had the news: his father had just come out of the hospital where his leg had been amputated. He had been through six operations for the blood clot in his left leg. On the seventh time when there was nothing more to do, nothing left to do, they amputated the leg. By the time Alex saw his father, it had been done.

On the Sunday he went to visit, his parents had started drinking earlier than usual and the morning had begun its stretch into one long day. Alex walked into the big old house, the house he had grown up in; he could taste the sweetness of being a boy, the thrill of playing with bottle caps, in those days when the weather was always nice even when it rained. He tried to remember when he had been too little to cross the street all by himself. but the picture had yellowed edges, a spooky monochrome.

He watched his mother sitting on that lime green chair she had gotten for ninety-nine dollars when Seaman's Furniture had opened in the mall. She clasped her right hand in her left and looked down at nothing. 'I was always afraid your father would stop loving me and how would I ever get through it—it never dawned on me that I would stop loving him first.'

Alex wished he had never been born.

'I remember the night they decided to cut his leg off. That night was even worse than the day they actually did it.'

Alex looked over her shoulder and could see that one of the streetlights had burned out; he looked out into a darkness that shouldn't have been there.

He chose instead to recall the hymn of boyhood when most kids had nicknames. Then you moved to a new block and your nickname became part of another time. He realized he never had a nickname that really stuck, no way of telling who he was and what he had been on the way there. Suddenly a nickname was very significant; he wanted one.

He thought of his father and how he didn't have two legs. He wondered how he would feel if it were him. But all he could think of while he tried to strum the shock was the beginning of yet another song, 'I hope that you are right for what is left of me. Someone else has claimed the best of me.' No, he would change that to 'forbidden games have claimed the very best of me.' 'The most of me.' 'The rest of me.' 'Played games with all of me.' He wondered if he should ask his mother for a piece of paper so he could write down the parts he liked.

And then he saw his father come in the room with no leg and a walker, his eyes overblown, outstretched. Alex's father was the kind of man who might have said, 'We would have lost the battle, son, if it hadn't been for me,' but he had never been in any war. He did come out with things like 'a lot of numerous holidays' or 'they should include that into . . .'. But when Alex saw his father, he forgot all the things about him that he couldn't stand. He just looked at the dangling space where his leg had been. His father had pinned up the pants leg of the leg that wasn't there. On his one foot was a black sandal, half of a pair he had gotten in Mexico City where they made soles out of rubber tires. Alex wondered where the other sandal was. Would he bother to shine one shoe? Does anyone care if the shoe of a man with one leg is shined?

'So, tell me what you think you have to be depressed about,' his father said, patting the leg that wasn't there.

'I'm not depressed, dad,' he said, shifting from side to side. 'I have a lot of things on my mind.'

'My underwear is wet all the time.'

Alex made himself think boyhood again. When he was about seven or eight he had gotten a gift for his

father's birthday with his mother's plaid stamps. It was
a wooden clock that looked like plastic which now
seemed sadder than if it had been something plastic that
looked like wood. But his father had never sent him a
birthday card or a card of any kind. He didn't even know
what his father's handwriting looked like. He longed for
that intimacy. He wondered how children survive the
minutes that made them adults. How do things get their
color, and then go on to weather us, rain on us, dry us off
and snow us in.

His mother had a habit of connecting almost every
remark with a celebrity. Now she was saying. 'They
found out in the hospital that your father had
diabetes—now he'll have to take an insulin shot every
day . . . just like Mary Tyler Moore.' Alex understood
that wanting to be a part of a family was only good until
you got there.

His father tried to sit in a chair, leaning forward,
planting some invisible force firmly ahead, trying to
hide the fact that he was no longer in command.

You're jealous of me, Alex wanted to say, but did not.
'Aren't you going to get a wheelchair, dad?'

'And who'll wheel me?'

Alex didn't know what to say anymore. You run out of
things to say to sick people so much faster than you
think you ought to. They know you know they're
coming apart.

Later his mother would tell Alex: 'They're thinking of
cutting away his collarbone because they think it's
pressing on an artery and has something to do with the
blockage in the leg. But,' she added confidently, 'you
don't really need a collarbone.'

'I thought if you had it, you needed it.' Alex had
visions of his father collapsing like a tree with no root.

He thought of the movie *Das Boot*—the sound of the
British navy destroyer searching out the German U-
boat. The captain took the sub lower but the destroyer
didn't give up. Alex could hear that sound now.
Relentless. Don't let them hear you. Don't let them
know you're there. Maybe they'll go away.

And Alex's father was thinking of those Sunday
mornings long ago when he was a boy who put on a
peach colored choir gown with brown cotton half
diamond shapes around the collar. Once he got to the
choir loft, he couldn't wait to get out. Away from the
round resonant thunderous burning of the choirmaster
who talked out against a hundred issues, homosexuality,
touching yourself, thinking dirty thoughts, forbidden
movies, dirty magazines; clean up your hearts, he was
always saying. He had been a soldier of a boy then, his
young life a splendid creation of its own. Now his skin
was stretched over old cheeks and hair combed back
grey and dying, a voice solemn with lack of color and the
walls come tumbling down.

Alex's mother had glided out of the living room into
the kitchen away from his father who had turned on the
television. Alex had followed her. He wished somebody
could pull out all the stops.

'Sex is the ultimate affection,' his mother was saying.
'For anyone who wants to hold back affection, that is the
ultimate holdout.' 'Women are so taken by words,' he
heard his mother saying sorrowfully. 'He called me his
"precious little girl" and it sounded so pretty, me being
fifty-four and him being so much younger.' Alex wished
she had been talking about his father, her husband, but
she was telling him about her boyfriend in New York. 'A
woman must believe she is loved and then convince a
man of it.' She smiled through her words and her smile

lit up her crow's feet. Alex hated her for trying to look thirty-five.

'He thinks I'm forty-six. It'a hard to watch your face sag little by little every day. You're always trying to find the right light. You lie about your age to yourself way before you lie to anyone else. The numbers just don't fit, Alex. It's all going nowhere fast. Everything good feels like it's already happened. Do you understand?

'The only thing I have ever been able to do well in my life has been to love. But I needed some honest love back and your father's idea of protection was throwing his hands up in the air and saying "case closed".' So you can see your father never said anything like "precious little girl" to me.'

Alex wanted to say 'You're drunk' but last time he had accused her of that, she had answered, 'Well, yes, I have been drinking, but I am not drunk.'

'I could never figure out if your father was in love with me and didn't know it or if he felt nothing and was guilty about that. I tried to stay detached but I still paid too much attention. I'm tired, Alex. I feel like I've spent a lifetime just standing around hoping someone would notice me.'

Alex thought of another song. 'Don't make me cry, I don't have time.' He knew he was living in an age where they were forever making heroes out of ordinary people; and so ordinary people keep getting decorated until someone asks why and the cheering stops.

And when he was leaving, his father, gesturing to what was no longer there, said, 'I'll never get used to this, you know. I'll never get used to this.'

Outside the rain had started and was furious. The wind sounded round and Alex watched how fast a bird can scoot to shelter.

CHAPTER TWELVE

Smile, They Tell Miss America

Here's what happened the last time Fiarette saw Alex.

'You're not happy and it's costing me. You either catch on to life or you don't, Alex.' Fiarette bit her lip at how tough she sounded and you could see it. She could tell by the look in his eyes that he was feeling the punches.

She didn't know how to tell him that she had picked up the shirt he left behind on the bathroom floor and felt sick at the way the yellow and white stripe was eaten away by the sweat under his arms. She didn't know how to tell him that being satisfied with living like a pig was a sign of weakness. She didn't know how to tell him that she hated when he called her 'my fair lady'. Everything about him was medium and she didn't know how to tell him that either. He had a strange habit of referring to the third person when in fact he was talking about one of them. Fiarette would yawn and he would say, 'She's tired,' or he would be in bed pounding inside of her and say, 'Alex doesn't want to come.'

Once in a while he would say something that wasn't medium like when he gave her the flowers that time and said, 'Flowers are the last living thing given to the dead.'

Those words had stunned her. And the time they were walking out of Washington Square Park and he had pointed high in the sky, 'That's Number One Fifth Avenue where Patti Smith used to live.'

'Ask me what I think about love, Alex,' Fiarette said.

So he asked her, 'What do you think about love, my fair lady?'

'I don't believe a word of it.' Her voice was flat. 'Maybe I learned early that love is not the answer. I'm not even sure we need love in our lives, except the songs keep telling us we do. What do you think it means to love and be loved? Do you think it means you'll have all the answers?'

'You mean me, right? You mean you don't really need me.'

'Oh, Christ, don't be so sensitive. You know, for a man, you're too sensitive. You want someone to hang on to.'

'I'm trying to stay honest.'

'I'm trying to stay honest, too, Alex. You're just not so totally important to me. If you were, then you would be everything and then life gets crowded. And crowds are dangerous. It's just a question of who gets hurt first. We both end up getting it after a while. I'm just trying to postpone the pain.

'Right now, I think I need distance, Alex. I'd rather fill my life with inanimate things.' Fiarette knew she really did want to hurt him. For one thing, she enjoyed knowing she could get away with it. She felt hard inside and the stupid lost look on Alex's face made her disgusted.

'What do you want, Fiarette?'

'I want to do it my way, Alex.' She felt both corny and bloodless.

'And I . . . I want to please you.'

'You're still fighting for your manhood, Alex, Christ, you'll probably never know what it means.' Whatever he felt, whatever little he was left with, she was determined to rob him.

'I hate the way you spin the dial on the radio until you find some stupid music you're ready for. You don't even turn the dial, you spin it. You take rice cakes out of the refrigerator and don't tie the wrapper back on. You leave the wrapper on one shelf and the rice cakes on another. And the way you lick your fingers after just about everything you eat. Then you take a shower and change the showerhead position and never put it back the way I like it. You always take the bar of yellow soap from the sink and leave it in the shower. I use strawberry bath soap and almond face soap; the bath soap goes in the bathtub and the face soap stays in the sink. But not according to you. Then you throw the towel over the side of the tub wringing wet instead of hanging it over the rod to dry.'

She tried to shut up, feeling cranky, crotchety, worried that she had forgotten how to live with other people. She hated their noises, their humming, their whistling, the way they chewed their gum, the way they breathed.

'And you make me feel like a bitch, Alex. Worse of all, you make me feel like a bitch. I hate the way every morning the first thing you say as soon as I open my eyes is "Did you have any dreams?"'

He sat there with a copy of *Rolling Stone* in his lap. He wanted to read the cover story on Eddie Murphy but after this outburst he figured he'd just leave.

After he left, she went into the bathroom; the butts of two cigarettes Alex had thrown in the toilet floated there. They made her sick. She flushed the toilet but the butts bubbled back. She spent the rest of the night talking to herself, turning on the television and watching Burt Reynolds in *The Longest Yard* and then throwing out a purple Indian cotton dress with a spot that just wouldn't come out. She realized she would never find a way to get rid of the spot and she would never wear it with the spot on it, not even around the house, so she might as well throw the dress out.

On the morning of July fourth, which that year fell on a Saturday, Martin Worthy sat at the small round oak table in his kitchen over a cup of black coffee. The mug was his favorite, thick ceramic, a fine red with a Christmas tree on it. The Christmas tree looked like the kind of Christmas tree you draw the first time you try to draw a Christmas tree. It had wide white candles at the tip of each branch. It had a white ball for a star. Martin remembered drawing Christmas trees as a boy—his stars were always five pointed and yellow.

And with his mug of coffee in his hand, he moved to the typewriter and began writing. Through it all, the whitewashed roads and the warmed over luck, Martin Worthy kept on writing. He did not know just where his story was going. But he never sensed peril. When he sat down to write, there was a playfulness to it, the rich understanding that his characters knew when to wake up and when to fall asleep and when to lie awake kicking and when to curl up in tears. They saw each other when the need arose. They got mad at each other when they had to. They were jealous; they were joyful. They knew their lines.

He wondered more about technical things—how many chapters should there be, should they be numbered, or just read like long passages, long informative sketches? How much should be narrative and how much dialogue? How would he know not to pay attention to things that got in the way? Should he use one sentence to describe something, or ten? And then suddenly the answers would come, an understanding so clear that this heart would feel full; without too many graphics, he would know how something should be said.

His favorite characters were the ones who never had enough money but more than enough wit.

CHAPTER THIRTEEN

The Gypsy Woman in *Frankenstein Meets the Wolf Man* says
'He is not insane. He simply wants to die.'

Everyone would be sure to remember the bon voyage
party that Joel gave on the roof of his Perry Street
apartment on July fourth; tomorrow he would fly to
Brussels and then go by train to Rome.

At dusk the air was a chorus of noise, blasts, spatters,
sputters and loud trembles. By eight o'clock it was dusty
grey, still light, and everyone was saving the special
fireworks for when it got real dark.

On the morning of July fourth Alex had woken up and
knew he was in trouble. He could feel the glory coming.
He wanted to talk to his brother Steve. He was thinking
how nice it would be if Steve and he and his father and
mother could sit together, maybe for Thanksgiving
dinner, or Sunday breakfast, anything, just to feel like a
family. When does a family stop being a family? He
understood the cruel stillness of it, people living in a
circus just because it had a roof. He was sure that if he
blinked he would be gone. He swallowed a downer,
stepped, not jumped, into a hot shower and trusted to
God. He got high fast and looked in the mirror. 'You
know what's going to kill me?' he told himself in the
mirror. 'My exhilaration.' That's what he told himself

when he left for the bon voyage party that no one would ever forget. Outside, he went into the corner deli and over to the freezer. He took out a can of Pepsi and the man behind the counter said, 'Ho, ho, ho, ready to take the Pepsi challenge.' He stepped over a gift box with Santa Claus wrapping paper still on it; it was the Fourth of July but Santa Claus seemed strangely relevant. Alex wondered how the box had gotten there; he wondered how he had gotten there.

On the way to the party Alex saw a car with a bumper sticker. He had no way of knowing the guy driving it had been to bed with his mother. The bumper sticker said 'Girls Just Wanna Have Fun.' He saw two pre-teen girls seduced by Haagen-daz ice cream and the summer heat. He heard two kids talking and one of them said his sister's boyfriend looked like a potato. It didn't make him laugh.

Ambition gives you something to do and an obsession is no fun if somebody tries to take it away from you. Those thoughts taken together made him feel like he had been erased, the vague displacement of being only half there. He kept on walking.

His perpetual clarity saw a world full of errors. Why, he wondered, was it so visible to him. Did anyone else spot the misspellings, the missteps, the misgivings, the plucky sadnesses, the graffiti on the wall: VICTOM OF CIRCUMSTANCE. A sign in a store: SUMMUR CLEARANCE. Something else said 'Two application per person.' In the subway was a sign 'Men room.' A grocery store on Ninth Avenue said 'EEGS 89¢ a dozen.' Life is a small world, Alex heard someone say. They were talking to someone else but he knew it was meant for him. The fatigued pulse of back stage.

Everywhere he walked he saw something miscast. It was driving him crazy.

OPEN FOR BREKFAST

CLERENCE SALE

The motorman on the shuttle had said 'Watch your steps.'

He thought of this line from Kurt Vonnegut's *Slaughterhouse Five.* 'How nice to feel nothing and still get full credit for being alive.' Alex understood fringe: Life would forever be a project. The motors of hell.

Then he saw this scratched on a wall.

Ron 'n Donna
Paul n' Michelle

and someone had added 'Drowning in Despair—Drip, Drop and Droop.'

On Twenty-Fifth Street: 'Mose vitamins reduced 25%' in a health store window.

And: 'Store close's at five.'

And 'Help the Homeless. God bles.'

A blue truck passed with a sign in those press-on letters from a hardware store: P L U M IN G.

Another: 'Necless—$2'.

SENSUOS. This was spelled out on a schoolyard wall with white paint that ended with a drip and the final 'u' missing. He hated graffiti that was misspelled. It was there forever, a permanent tactical error.

Didn't anybody go to school anymore?

The party was on the roof of a six story apartment building. The first breeze of the day had come up about

five-thirty and the day's heavy heat hung still in the air.
Alex arrived wearing a satin New York Yankees baseball
jacket that he had gotten at So Cheap on Broadway. He
wore it over a pair of gym shorts and told the first person
he bumped into that he was planning to go to New
Zealand when the summer was over.

'You know what Ricardo did,' someone couldn't wait
to tell him. 'He forged a check of his girlfriend's for two
hundred dollars to buy two grams of coke. And then he
did the whole thing himself even though he promised to
share it with Jonathan, the math major he lives with.
Jonathan swears he never saw it.'

'Jonathan's no math major. He's a make-up artist,'
someone said.

'He's both.'

Alex was thinking about cruise missiles, intermediate
range rockets, and how they are designed to fly low to
evade radar detection.

Somewhere Fiarette was trying to understand what
happened to those days when she took pride in being
kind, in making other people's lives more happy than
her own, the mystery of idealists. But the truth was she
never wanted to see Alex again.

Alex moved off into a corner for a while. Up on the
roof the tops of the buildings looked higher than they
really were; there was more sky than anything else.
Cone shaped, flat topped, they grew, grey, brown and
clay, into the sky. Alex studied the windows, so many of
them, rectangular solitary spaces, as varied as the
buildings. In the distance he saw a clockface and a
weathervane. He began thinking about that summer
when he worked as a stock boy in a hosiery company in
the Empire State Building and a sailor leaped off the
observation deck. The next day a left arm was found on

the canopy of Ohrbach's Department Store right across Thirty-Fourth Street. Alex remembered how he had made it a point to look for blood on the sidewalk the next lunch hour, but he found none. He wished he could have seen this happening. Did the sailor splatter? Did he come apart in the air?

The tar was hot on his feet as he walked over to the north side of the roof; the ledge was about four feet high. He looked over. The antique store on the corner had two evergreens in cement pots; they were dying in the July heat. On the roof of one of the brownstones was a few hundred feet of thick rusty chain coiled in a heap. On another roof a yellow sheet and a red sheet hung out to dry next to each other. Down in a doorway stood a girl with a long pony tail and khaki shorts with her back to the street. Cars and lazy trucks passed, slow holiday traffic. People strolled through it. Two girls and a guy with a camera hooked around his shoulder. The breeze came up. A woman in red and white stripes sat on a deck chair on another roof top. A magazine was in her lap and nearby was an empty blue baby carriage.

He edged toward the other end of the roof where the ladder hooked over the side; here the ledge was much lower than four feet, maybe even less than two feet. His knees shook. He could see death, could feel his head being stuffed in a plastic bag, could see them cutting his body down from a poisonous looking ragged rope; his eyes were his face and there was no smile anywhere. He was too afraid to look over, but not too afraid to jump.

In less time than it took a New York City sanitation truck to empty the garbage from the north side of the street, Alex finalized it once and for all in his head and was dead. Life was a whir, death was forever, and he was glad to be gone.

Later they would argue about who was the first to know that Alex had taken the quick and easy.

His friend Elliott felt the tears. 'He didn't know how to shift the blame.'

In Alex's pocket on a piece of lined paper folded in four were the words to what Alex knew was his best song:

> She had a face of an angel in reverse
> And a heart with a mighty bit more
> And close to the ground
> Was where she could be found
> That was all that she wanted to love.

A truck that said New York City Health and Hospitals Mortuary came and took him away. One of the two men in the truck took off Alex's dirty white leather sneakers and left them on the sidewalk not far from the curb. Later on someone threw them in the garbage. A girl at the party who had been taking pictures with her new Nikon autofocus camera had run out of film by the time Alex got there. And that night someone would recall Alex had always rolled such nice fat joints.

CHAPTER FOURTEEN

After You've Gone And Left Me Crying

You think of the people you love at the damndest times. Cutting open a melon for lunch listening to the radio about people leaving organs after their death. Katherine Hepburn pleading for eyes for corneal transplants. Fiarette was thinking of Alex. She remembered that he did have an organ donor card and she hoped he hadn't left his eyes. She wondered what she would do if she saw them on somebody else.

The terrible thing was that no one could really say anything great about Alex. A lot of people loved him but no one knew why. Perhaps in the end we all become broken promises and bad debts. Potential is a buzz word and life is a pep talk.

But Fiarette brooded more and more often. She wondered about her capacity for happiness—was it even there anymore? She began to forget what was going on around her because she became part of it, caught up in the motion of detachment. The state of mourning was a state of siege, a final, sizable verdict.

Alex had said to her once, 'If you know you're going to lie, just say "I don't want to talk."' His eyes had been bright, extraterrestrial, his voice soft.

'I don't feel like myself anymore,' she told Kary. 'I can no longer explain myself. It's been like this ever since Alex died.'

The day after he died she dug out of her bureau drawer a black ribbed t-shirt with a pink rose appliqué on it. She hadn't worn it for a few years, but she wanted to wear something of yesterday.

'I can't believe you're not going to the funeral,' Kary had said.

'Why should I go? He won't be there.' That was how it felt to Fiarette. The funeral would be a strenuous journey to see someone who wasn't there. And she was sure that she would never be able to think of Alex without wanting to stop everything and cry; just thinking about it, her tears were everywhere. And she began hating people because they didn't know when to shut up. She longed for quiet, the stillness of pages slowly being turned.

All of a sudden there was this dullness inside her—he was dead and she realized she had adored him.

Alex dead, his grace gone. It made her sick every time she thought about it. She stayed out on the street as long as she could; walking aimlessly freed her from decision. She understood that she had been the worst of all things: a nag, who tortured his integrity by insisting on her own way.

Alex kept turning up. She opened the refrigerator and found a bottle of Colt 45. She remembered how every time Alex finished a Colt 45 he always put the bottle cap on before he tossed the bottle away.

She knew she'd never see him again, but it would have been easier if he hadn't left his blue sweatshirt behind. She didn't know whether to wash it or to leave it just the way it was. She knew she couldn't throw it away so she folded it neatly in a drawer with her nightgowns.

'Be loving and you will be loved,' her therapist had once told her. But all she could remember was the time she told Alex, 'When I dance I don't like people to put their hands on me until I put my hands on them first.'

And Fiarette's anger knew no bounds. She was not upset because she had hurt Alex; she was upset that she was upset. She was upset that he could still upset her. She did not want to drown in guilt because Alex Chase's silly music was no more to be heard. She did not want to take the blame because once the burden of guilt was hers, changes would have to be made.

By ten-thirty in the morning she had started three things and had finished none of them. Her dress lay on the bed, fully pinned but half hemmed. A letter to a girl she had gone camping with in Port Antonio fourteen years ago lay written, but unmailed. Everything was for her a version of what it had been before. She had half her clothes on, socks but with bedroom slippers, a bra and a t-shirt. If anything had more than two steps or three parts, she couldn't go through with it.

Outside now she walked aimlessly behind two guys in a spirited conversation. 'You gotta see the video,' one of them said impatiently.

In the park Fiarette found plenty of seats around the fountain and sat back and wondered why the fountain had never been turned on all summer; there was no water shortage; as a matter of fact, there had been too much rain.

A good looking guy with some dried blood on his face came up to her.

'You don't mind if I sit here?'

She nodded either yes or no, the ambiguity of deadly indifference.

'Thanks. Thank you very much.' He sat down.

'If I nod out, miss, would you mind just tapping me here on the shoulder. Or,' he continued, 'if anyone comes over and starts bothering me, just give me a rap on the arm.' He pointed to the arm she should rap on and began to nod out. He continued mumbling as he continued nodding out. 'I hope I'm not interfering with you or anything, because I'm on eighty milligrams and it would really be nice if you could talk to me.'

'I don't talk.'

'What's your name anyway.'

Fiarette got up and moved to the other end of the fountain.

Three kids passed by, hair punked up. 'I have to take the LL and then a bus to get home,' one says. Another is out of it. The third one saw Fiarette out of the corner of his eye and stops. 'Let's stop here,' he says to his friends, 'this looks like a good location.'

'Location?' Fiarette thought. 'Location?'

She sat there wondering how long it would be before he said something. She could feel him sitting real close to her, the husky blonde one.

'Do you want to get high?'

She doesn't answer.

'Don't you want to enjoy yourself?'

'I am enjoying myself.'

'So what do you think of sex?'

She ignored him and he turned away. They get up to go but the third one has fallen asleep and they can't move him.

'I feel like a hero,' one says.

'I feel like a beer.'

'Let's sprint around.'

They try to move their friend.

'Miss, would you mind just watching him for us while we go get a beer?'

'I'm not watching him. I don't want that responsibility.'

'You know, just in case he wakes up, tell him we'll be right back.'

'He won't wake up for a long time,' Fiarette tells them.

'You live around here? You know people around here?' says one.

'You live in the neighborhood?' says the other.

'Yes, I live around here.'

'Oh, yeah? Do you know anyone on Macdougal Street?'

'Do you know the DiFrancos?'

'Look,' Fiarette says, 'I don't feel like talking. Can't you see that I just don't feel like talking.'

Death had sobered her, poked her, made her powerless in a world where everything is marginal and the rains keep coming and the people you love are gone, washed away, and their absence is more and more bewildering.

She found a piece of paper with the name of the funeral parlor on it and the hours: seven to ten. Monday night. She didn't want to see the body. She just wanted images: casual smoky images of Alex, full-blown lips saying: 'Where you been all my life?' Alex trying to teach her to trust her sense. Vigorous intellectual images, like Alex calling life 'a parallel existence'.

CHAPTER FIFTEEN

An Adventure is Where
You Don't Know What's Going to Happen

The person who did go to the funeral parlor was Kary. She thought the dizzy scrutiny of seeing Alex in the coffin would give her a renewed addiction to life. And it was there that Steve came over and told her, 'Our real father died when I was eight months old. Alex was three years older than me, but I always felt older than him. He got picked on, but I got ignored.' Kary looked at the man in the wheelchair who she thought looked too old to be married to Alex's mother. Steve pointed to a black minister standing close to the door. 'And Alex was raped by him. He and his wife and daughter are still close friends of my mother. Weird, right?' He switched gears. 'I'm living with this guy in the East Village. He lets me stay there as long as I give him my food stamps. He's a guy from Queens named Gary, but he bleached his hair and started calling himself Todd.

'Alex always felt people knew something about him that he didn't know himself, something he was still struggling with. The more he fought it, the stronger it got in him. There were just too many things he didn't know how to talk about.'

'I only met Alex once,' Kary told him.

'Then why are you here?'

'I thought I needed to be reminded of death.' She did not look into his eyes when she said it. But it came out straight, flat and honest.

'Life is depressing, but we all fit right in,' Kary told him. 'I was walking down Fourteenth Street today and I saw a kid with a toy, a monster made out of this ugly purple velveteen. He pushed it into his mother's face. "Smell it," the kid said. It made me laugh. There's so many things happening out on the streets that make me laugh. I was stoned, so I guess that helped. Then I went in the deli to pick up a bagel with cream cheese. The guy said, "Do you want to take it out?" I kind of lost it there for a minute. "Take out means I don't want to have it here, right?" "Right." Then I said, "Then I want to take it out."'

That made them smile at each other.

The next night Kary called Steve because she wanted company. He told her: 'I think friends should be more than just people to go places with. Just like I think women should be more than just people to sleep with.'

Kary wasn't sure whether or not she liked that angle. It was the kind of negative suggestion that would stay with her and have her chain smoking at bedtime. It made her feel like maybe she was starting to look like something that got caught in the rain. It made her feel low. She liked the way he looked.

'I have no plans,' was all she found she could say. The less said, the better; communicating had to mean more than just words. She was testing Steve to see if he really knew how to talk. Fiarette always could communicate with her; she alone understood Kary's most abstract sentiments.

'Does that have anything to do with what I just said about women being more than people to sleep with?' Steve asked.

'If you like.'

And some of the confidences they told each other:

From Steve: 'Once I was addicted to valium and painkillers for back pain. One night I woke up sitting in the middle of the floor with a broken lamp in my hands.'

From Kary: 'I used to be real close to my father. He always kept a picture of me in an oval silver frame on his desk at work. It was a picture of me just the way I wanted to look, just the way I hope I'll look every time I look in the mirror, not smiling too hard, but looking happy. I always loved him for that. It's great to have someone want to look at your picture all day. He divorced my mother a few years ago. He took me to Spain to break the news to me. I asked him what his new girlfriend was like and he told me, "She looks good in pants."'

Steve was looking at her eyes and decided they were too close together. But he liked the way she moved like a cat.

'Now,' Kary went on, 'I have a crush on my mailman. I think it's because he looks like a father. Not my father, just a father. He has a daddy's face and he's just the right size.

'My problem is I want all the right things, only I seem to want them too much. Love is usually what does us in. That's the hard part. When I was sixteen, I had all my babies' names picked out. All seven or eight of them. I couldn't imagine anything better than wheeling a baby carriage around with one of those satin pillows with the baby's name in flowing script on a ribbon. I wanted lots of babies, around my ankles, pulling at my hair, bobbing in my lap, cradled in my arms. It was always such a clear picture.'

And Steve said, 'The best thing about the past is you forget what could have made you happy. That's from *Lovers and Other Strangers*.'

Kary kept looking at him, trying to decide if he was cute. Then she said, 'I meet a lot of guys with money but hardly any who have class. Some people really love money, but I'm different. I like having no money. I play a game sometimes. How far can I go with five dollars in three days. For a dollar you can buy five oranges or three bagels or sixteen ounces of plain yogurt. Lacto plain is seventy-nine cents and Breyers is ninety-three. Or you can get a head of lettuce and three small peppers. Clothes don't mean a thing to me, either. My idea of fashion is to make sure I never get caught dead carrying a savings bank shopping bag.'

Steve was watching her, a globe in space, and thinking things he hadn't thought in a long time. He was wondering how the material of her skirt would feel in his hands. It would sizzle.

'I'm a pretty gloomy person. Do you know the difference between depression and gloom? Gloom has less pep. The last time I smiled was when I saw *Snow White*.'

'Why are you so gloomy?' Steve asked her.

'I guess it's because I talk myself out of my feelings. I don't want to be miscast and I don't want to be misled. Gloomy means it's okay to wait.' She was a rough bundle.

The next night they went dancing. Steve didn't have any drugs so Kary said she would give him a black beauty. He told her over the phone that he didn't feel like climbing up six flights of stairs to Kary's apartment;

could they meet downstairs and could she bring a cup of water for him to take his black beauty? The cup she brought down was a Miss Piggy cup that said: 'Smile. It helps to stir up the fun.' She didn't feel like climbing back upstairs so she hid the cup under the stairs because it didn't fit in the mailbox.

In the corner of the disco a bunch of black kids had taken a small container of baby powder and spilled it all over the dance floor so feet could go sliding in the powder and really hum. Kary spun her body around the dance floor and felt like she was in heaven. Steve looked like he was slowing down way before she was ready to, but she let him take her into a corner away from the music and the smell of baby powder in the air.

'I was almost married once,' Steve told her. 'It killed me when it didn't work. She collected butterflies. Did you ever know anyone who collected butterflies?'

'No.'

'Neither had I. She was really special.'

Kary didn't want to hear about it, so she popped up and headed for the dance floor and said, 'Music, Maestro, let's get wet.'

Another weekend they spent sitting in the park. Pigeons with red feet bobbed towards them, chattering. 'Do pigeons concentrate?' Kary asked Steve. She watched a black breasted pigeon pecking at itself. Margie, the old lady, sat next to them in the park, blue penny loafers on her feet; her blouse was see-through grey white cotton tucked inside pastel cruisewear. Kary was sure she got all dressed up just to come to the park. A mosquito buzzed around her ankles and she stopped to shake him away. She had a golden brown cane the color of an ochre Crayola. She wore heavy dark nylons in the August heat and picked at peanut shells with the tip of her cane. She had a day-old copy of the *New York Times* which she had separated, sitting on one half and slipping the other half behind her neck, sliding it over the weathered rough planks of the park bench. She strained to see a baby in red sleeping in a baby carriage. 'Look,' she said to Kary, eyeing a squirrel with a peanut. 'Look,' she said again, as the policemen opened the doors of their patrol car to keep cool. Age meant not wanting to miss a thing.

A can of Coors was at Steve's feet. Across from them a man held a radio in his lap with both hands and a plastic shopping bag from The Wiz was at his feet. The shadows shaded his tanned cheeks and lit up his eyes. The sound was so low that not even he could hear it.

A kid with blue satin gym shorts and a cap pitched sideways on his head called to the sanitation man hosing down the grass. 'Yo! Wet me.' The kid thrashed his arms around and the man flashed the power spray at him, and he jumped up and down in the jet of water.

In early August they put grass in the park, mats of bright green fuzz. They raked the old and resod the new, which arrived piled high on a flat-bed truck on its way back to the earth.

Kary watched kids going up the sliding pond backwards. The sun reflected off a metal disc and got caught in her eye.

Later they went to Steve's. His room sat small in a pale corner of the building that got no sun. A table poked one corner of the room, choking it.

On the t.v. screen they were flashing the phone number of the Bat Patrol of the New York City Police Department. They played the Batman theme while they showed a bat being captured in someone's home in the Pelham Parkway section of the Bronx.

'This place has all the excitement of an empty beer can,' Steve said. And Kary was wondering if she shouldn't cut her hair and move. But where?

CHAPTER SIXTEEN

She was at that stage where she knew
she either had to throw out some clothes
or get some more hangers

That night Kary and Fiarette sat in Kary's kitchen. 'I hate mushrooms,' Kary was telling Fiarette; she stirred something in her soup.

Fiarette looked at the label on the empty soup can. 'Then why did you buy Mushroom Barley Soup?' she said in capital letters.

'Because I didn't think there'd be so many of them. And the can was so high on the shelf I almost broke my arm getting it down.'

Fiarette sighed and said, 'So what about last night?'

'I don't know how it happened. We were at his apartment. He was staring at me and telling me I was a sexy woman. We were sitting at his table. He rolled a joint. Then he moved the ashtray to one side and moved a newspaper to the other side and took my hand and held it on the table and I knew he meant business. And the next morning he brought me breakfast and then he went shopping—to buy maybe shorts or maybe shoes. How does it happen?' She shrugged with her voice. 'It happens.'

'He's gay, Kary.'

'Oh, don't be ridiculous. He told me I tasted good.

Just because you have red hair, you think you're God.'

Fiarette wanted to stop right there, but she couldn't. 'I'm telling you, Kary, he's gay.'

'You're trying to free yourself from too many excesses, Fee. Life is what you make it, not what it is.'

'Well, you go ahead and live by your wits, Kary. I'm afraid to.'

'There was a time when all I needed to make me happy was ten dollars so I could go dancing,' Kary said, suddenly getting mopey.

'Ten dollars . . . excluding the price of the drugs,' Fiarette loped in.

Kary ignored her. 'Then I could dance and dance all Saturday night and drink fruit juice and dance and dance some more and get the *Times* on Sunday morning and come home and go through the whole thing, section by section.'

It was only when they were both stoned that it seemed they could have a good time, whatever 'good time' might mean on a particular day. Just the two of them wasn't always good enough. Getting high was what they always did when they were together. She tried to remember ever having a friend she could enjoy, really enjoy, when they were both cold sober. She knew it would have to have been a long time ago, kids jumping rope, cutting circle skirts out of bright bolts of fabric from the five and ten, collecting stamps, learning that stamps marked Norsk were from Norway and stamps marked Helvetia were from Switzerland, buying turtles with your name painted on their shell.

'I told Steve how I'm always afraid of getting lost in Central Park and he told me that the little footpaths leading out of the park always run parallel to the wide paths. I always feel like I'm the last one to find out about things like that.'

Fiarette was wondering what it would be like to be so famous that you had to have an unlisted phone number.

'His apartment was a mess. He said it was a good thing I wasn't allergic to dust or else I'd be blown away. And then somewhere into the night he said, "Are you easy to get into bed?" And I said, "Try me" and then,'—she smiled wide, 'and then . . . the bus tore through the countryside.'

And Fiarette was thinking like this: 'I used to be able to pay more attention for longer periods of time.'

'My mother used to always say, "Kary, why can't you be normal?" And I'd say, "maybe it's not normal for me to be normal."'

And Fiarette was thinking how it had never been much of a friendship. Kary talked and she listened. Kary ranted and she watched. Life was a series of repetitions for Kary—men and jobs. She was always planning to leave once she got there.

CHAPTER SEVENTEEN

How was Las Vegas?
It was hot, 111 degrees. But we had a good time.
We saw Paul Anka and Wayne Newton
and took pictures in front of Caesar's Palace.

Martin Worthy wanted to get his story down. He wanted to see if it worked. It was like a courtship you hoped would lead to marriage, but you had to go through all the steps to learn about vision.

He wanted this girl he was creating with his words to meet the man of her dreams. But the man of your dreams only got that way because you made him that way, molding and shaping him in the image and likeness of God. So he needed a girl with enough charm who knew how to do this, who knew how to compel a man to be what she needed, to teach him how to recover from memory.

Ah, he was beginning to feel like a writer. He allowed himself the liberty of his vast moods. He assumed he would be forgiven for an occasional crankiness. He was exhilarated by the thought of eccentricity.

He understood words as never before. The sadness that had so filled him like a swamp was beginning to even out. He saw words as meanings that could be shaded, decorated, lyrical smoke. He was hooked into a source of light like the beam of a flashlight. He was a bright raft in blue waters.

As a writer he was learning that you never say, 'I will write twenty pages in three hours.' You say, 'I will allow myself to write twenty pages, at my own pace. As long as by the time I go to sleep, I have twenty pages of my writing.'

He was not afraid of anything because he now understood that he had the ability to review fear and comment on it. He conquered it by putting it on paper. He gave other people his fears and then he showed them what to do to make them go away. He could take swipes at mankind and no one would know it was him. He ambled through vast luxurious lobbies. He borrowed faces from streets of dreams and put words in their mouths. His soul mattered more than his face; he forgot how much money he had in the bank or what he ate for dinner the night before or to pick up a pair of shoes at the shoemaker or to drop off dirty laundry.

And wherever he went, he began to listen for the hum of a room. He wanted his words to be understood but he didn't really care who thought what of him. He wanted to remain a sweet mystery. He would swoon over himself and delight in his ability to splice, to clip, to mesh, to blend; sitting at his typewriter, typed pages to the left of him, his legal yellow pads in front of him, his many pencils to the right of him, he felt absolutely balmy.

And when it was over he lay on his bed exhausted, the words stopped. Where? That mighty stream to the fragile trickle? What made the thrill of emotion, the spray of fire, run in reverse? What motives, past and present, slowed it down?

He had a folder for his notes on chapter breakdowns and on the front of it he pasted a picture from a newspaper of a license plate that said 'I'd rather be fishing.' But he was only kidding. Sometimes the room smelled like stale wine. The wallpaper was peeling top and bottom and there were places where the dirt was caught forever. But the specialness set in and all he wanted to do was write.

He did not know where these people came from, paintings in his head, chronicles of relevancy. Suddenly they were there, as clear as if they were knocking on a door, jumping up at the back of a crowd, waving hands in a crowded room, shouting, here I am, pick me!

And he laughed as he wrote about them. 'You need me to reinforce your illusions,' he said to the long yellow pad.

CHAPTER EIGHTEEN

Some lines from Edna St. Vincent Millay:
With him for a sire and her for a dam
what should I be but just what I am?

Somewhere there is spring and gardens are growing. It was a nice thought, but simple poetry bewildered Kary's consciousness. For Kary, life was there but not for her. Life was for the living. For her it was limited rage.

She was in a scattered mood, trying to do a number of things at once, not because she was rushed—she had plenty of time because she never planned much of anything—but because she never understood the dignity of parting company with yourself. On full-scale days she could not concentrate long enough even to lace up her sneakers. This morning had been one of those. She decided she didn't like the red laces she had put on her white Adidas sneakers, the pair with three red stripes on the side. The sneakers had come with white laces and now she realized she should have left them that way. She started to unlace the red lace on one sneaker to replace it with the original white. But she had staying power for only one shoe. Then she lay it down and went into the bathroom and tossed soap flakes in the bathroom sink and washed out the yellow shirt she had spilled something on last Saturday night. Then she heated water for coffee but when the steam hissed she shut the kettle,

no longer wanting coffee because by then she had
decided to roll a joint. She had defrosted the refrigerator
last night so she filled the kitchen sink with hot water to
wash out the butter dish and vegetable bins. Then she
decided to get two empty glass jars out of the closet and
put popcorn in one and rigatoni in the other. Then that
thought was gone because she put the jars in the sink to
be washed. By then she had decided to iron the few
dresses she had washed a couple of nights before. She
pulled out the ironing board from between the brooms
and the mop and filled the iron with hot water and
plugged it in. She set it to permanent press because
Fiarette had told her you can never burn anything at
permanent press. She went in to the bathroom to bring
out the dresses that had been hanging over the shower
rod. She went to iron the baby blue one with the
scalloped white flowers and saw that it had a big spot on
the bottom; she had hung it next to a rose pink cotton
dress, also wet, that had stained it. So she decided to see
if she could hem the stained part. So she left everything
and went to find some white thread. Then she realized
she didn't really feel like getting out the pins and the
measuring tape but she didn't want to put the dress
away because then she'd forget all about the stain. So
she threw it over a chair. About then she felt like taking
the red laces out of the second sneaker. Immediately
after that she read an article on power walking. And
then she put the white laces in the second sneaker. In
that order. And then she was filled with a sudden desire
to look at the photographs of the day she and Fiarette
had taken the bus to Asbury Park. Kary could always
gauge the state of her mental health by how many things
she did not bother putting away in her apartment.
Sometimes she wanted something really badly and

wouldn't pull it out because it meant climbing up to the top of her closet. She hated not being able to get to something. It always felt like everything she wanted was on top of something else. But she climbed up on the footstool and pulled down the album with the pictures from Asbury Park. There was Kary in her straw hat with the wide red band, sitting on a rock with Convention Hall in the background and a can of coke in the foreground. There was a starfish in her album and the wrapper from the Berkeley Sweet Shop on the Boardwalk and a picture of Kary against a wall of hats in a souvenir shop, and a picture of Fiarette and Fiarette's reflection in a store window.

She could feel it coming, the depression, a song that was too sad. Her lips felt frozen in her face—a face pastoral with seduction—and the tears were there, flowing, to rescue the soul, but from what. All she was doing was reading a department store sales folder, as a matter of fact, and all it said was: 'Fifty per cent off imported fine china service for four. "Happiness Grey" has a grey border with pink and blue floral, white ground, four each dinner, soup, salad, cup and saucer.' But depression was the nonsense of horror with a mind of its own.

She had not visited her family for months now, yet she was not eager to hurry home; she knew the person it was time for was her mother, but that was a face she did not even want to look at. When anyone would ask her what her mother was like, she would say, 'Mother has money, mother has men.' That's what mother was like. But it was from her mother that she needed confirmation that her deficits could be understood and her debts forgiven. Her mother wanted to change her from as far back as she could remember, never realizing what she wanted to change was a lumbering smile her daughter was born with; it did not allow for switching channels, but it did allow her to live by the vague weight of faith.

Her mother existed happily in trauma, her own and everyone else's. Life was confrontation and pretension. She knew all the stages of everyone's cancer. She thought life was mainly about decorating yourself and would never understand that raggedy panties were sexy as long as they smelled good. She had never been alone in her life except for a four and a half hour train trip and then her sister was waiting at the other end. She had a friend who did six thousand dollars worth of coke last year.

At that very moment Kary's mother was rubbing eye cream on her throat because she figured if it was good for her delicate eyes, it must be even better for the throat. She had ended dinner that night by saying to her latest boyfriend over his five course meal, 'How can you eat any more? You're going to bust.' She had left the table in the restaurant with repulsion on her face.

And when Kary walked into the house, her mother was on the telephone and Kary could hear only one side of the conversation, which went like this:

'Well, what else is there to do besides look pretty?' followed shortly by

'He never knew what he was doing in bed anyway.'

Kary just stood there waiting for her to get off the phone.

When she did, she announced, 'Oh, that was a friend of mine. She just found out her mother has cancer. Stage Four.'

And in the gaping silence of sudden death, Kary mumbled, with a twist, 'Mom, I really wanted to tell you about this guy.'

Her mother's eyebrows got higher and her voice was suspended mystique: 'Is it serious?'

'I guess so. He's moving in.'

She wanted to say something like, 'Ma, why is it that I think about sex all the time while other women think about recipes and skirt lengths and putting dust ruffles on their beds? Why is it the more I come, the more I want to?' She was after the prestige of options.

'Do you remember Lydia?' her mother asked. 'That pig who was a senior flight attendant at one of the airlines? She called me the other night and said she had done this terrible thing. Well, it turned out all it was that she was having an affair and she was leaving her husband. She was afraid the phone was tapped. She thinks she's pregnant and wanted to know if there was such a thing as night sickness because she couldn't keep down a thing but ginger ale.'

It was a Class B movie. There was no longer any certainty that one size fits all. Kary listened to a staggering melody. She did not know quite what it was, so she planted her feet firmly into the roots of the carpet and still felt shaky. She hated her mother. Her mother made friends with everyone and hobbled happily with their problems. Kary was suspicious of bound and gagged emotions and people who couldn't come up with one appropriate quotation.

The phone rang again and again she heard her mother's side of the story.

'She stayed with him through seventeen years of marriage and he didn't even love her. She gave up so much for him and he never loved her, not even back then. She never said to him that she shouldn't help with the money.'

Followed shortly by:

'I don't ask too many questions now. I try to stay out
of it. When I needed to ask him things, he never knew
the whole story. He wanted to keep tabs on them so they
wouldn't disappear into thin air.'

Followed shortly by:

'If he had a good social life, he wouldn't worry so
much about working at the post office.'

Her voice was a groan that had changed little in thirty
years, the voice of someone buying Bandaids at a drug
store. She gave her dentist a mug that said: 'Dentists
may lose their pull but never their polish.'

She was off the phone now and walking towards her
daughter again. 'This man I'm going out with is making
me sick, Katherine. He still, no matter what I say, uses
coasters for ashtrays and goes from window to window
pulling the blinds up and letting the sunshine in.
Sometimes I just don't feel like sunshine, damn it.

'So what's his name, the one who's moving in with
you?'

'Steve, mom, Steve.'

'And he's moving in?'

Kary nodded wearily. Barricades were never strictly
for laughs.

'Well, I guess your life can't be much more unhappy
than it is right now. I always told you to try and be more
cheerful.'

Kary's eyes felt their way around the room and she
knew she was going from lonely to distraught. She
thought of the time when she was a little girl and spied
through a window to see the super burn some kittens in
the basement boiler room of the big apartment building
across the street from where they lived. His name
was Mr Longstreet and all the kids called him Mr
Shortavenue. The distant past was deafening white

noise and a spring collection all at the same time.

Mother always wanted her to be like her friend Barbara who lived in that apartment building across the street, Barbara who was the first in the high school graduating class to get married, who had six children in as many years so that by the time she was twenty-four she was exhausted but still a practicing Catholic.

Kary wanted short pleasures in new grooves.

CHAPTER NINETEEN

The first murder ever to occur at Disneyland
was a corporate executive who was murdered
in the section of the park known as Tomorrowland.

Margie, the old lady in the neighborhood, was sitting in her kitchen, white on white, thinking, 'When I can't reach what I want in the supermarket, I reach for what I can get. That's why I'm sitting here eating a can of Chunky Chicken Vegetable when what I really wanted was Mushroom Barley.

'I am eighty-three years old today and I have learned the irony of such things as not being able to reach for what you want on a supermarket shelf. I am sitting in a kitchen thinking about supermarket shelves and a young man I once knew in the days when I knew young men who told me he spent a month in Hawaii and saw a rainbow every day.'

CHAPTER TWENTY

"I felt a strange sense of relief
As I let my mind collapse."
*Frances Farmer after being committed
for a second time to the sanitorium*

At work Fiarette sat sipping coffee and wanting more sugar in it. The subject of conversation was Cissy's hickey. Cissy herself had started the discussion by announcing she had a hickey but it wasn't where you could see it, quickly and gleefully adding that it was on her tit.

The subject shifted to the lawyers: who had the sexiest smile, who had the broadest back, who you'd most like to go to bed with and what you'd most like to do there.

Fiarette said nothing, but for the first time she realized there was only one man in that office she had ever looked at as other than a successful image maker—David Pond. She wondered how he would feel if he knew he was being thought of as a sex object. She knew that like any other man he wouldn't mind it at all. The flames would roar and the cheers would be hot. Then she realized with a jolt that she had wanted him from the minute she had first seen him. He had always looked good. Even though his work was practically illegible. He was so afraid of his documents getting lost in the inter-office mail that he made xeroxes of everything and kept the originals for himself. The print on the xeroxes was often uneven, with the ends of words trailing off the margins. He worked with the same group of attorneys and his drafts had all their handwritten inserts and everyone seemed to try to change what the person before him had wanted to say. Pages of it.

She decided then and there that starting the next day she would use the same coat closet he used—it was way down at the end of the long corridor she was at the other end of. There were two coat closets a lot closer, but she understood the odds of seeing him up close were better if they used the same closet. She contemplated leaving a pack of gum in her coat pocket so she could use that as an excuse to pay extra visits to the coat closet through the course of a day (a half stick of gum at a time) and maybe bump into him coming or going. She wondered what it would take for him to notice her. She longed for some hint of interest from him—but he was so low key it was like he wasn't there at all.

She felt like a fool on fire and willed herself to think of other things. Back to the conversation for ten minutes of tradition. Cissy had resumed discussing her hickey.

Fiarette got up from the couch in the ladies room, groaned at the sign above the Tampax machine, 'This machine owes me a dime,' and went back to her desk and put her head in her machine manual. It seemed there was always something in that manual she still had trouble understanding. 'Touch the SPACE bar to high-light the first document above the first column of numbers.' The machine made her feel like she was lining up suspended holes. There was the refusal to cooperate. She read on. 'A CODE 5 is used to center a heading OVER a column instead of between the margins. For example, if the largest number is 2,345 you must have at least five spaces between the tab and the special tab. If you set a regular tab at ten, then the number two would be at position ten, the comma at eleven, the three at twelve, the four at thirteen, and the five at fourteen. You would then set the special tab one position below to the right of the last number or at fifteen as shown below.'

She thought she was going crazy. Everything flunked.

That night she told Kary about David Pond. 'I wan't to wrap him around my finger. I want him to wrap me around his finger. I want to submit. I want to surrender. I want to throw myself at his feet. It's so close I can smell it.'

Meanwhile, Martin Worthy was writing and tossing the words he couldn't use right on the floor—the half sentences, the incomplete thoughts too old for completion, the likenesses that didn't work. Life and writing were full of illicit revisions. It felt so right to crumble paper into a ball and throw it on the floor.

He was writing every day, the obscure renegade, a decisive toughness in his stomach. He was thinking about remorse, part age and part anger, so many wrong turns and too few piano lessons where people and love become enemies and turn us against ourselves.

He was remembering the wide wooden boards on the bed he had slept in as a boy in the bedroom he shared with his sister. In between the beds was a night table with a radio on it and a picture of St Theresa who his sister was named after. On that radio they listened to 'Let's Pretend', 'Archie,' 'Sky King', 'Luigi', 'My Friend Irma', until television came in and he began to watch television but never lost an honest passion for the wonders of radio. The bed had come from one relative and the bed boards from someplace else and the boards never quite met the wooden slats under the bedsprings. Lots of times the slightest misplaced movement would send a slat sliding and a board tumbling and then the spring and the mattress would collapse and topple in a heap.

He realized he was scarcely looking at what he was typing; he was looking through it. He was being distracted by everything, the black handle of the scissors, the way his pens looked lined up next to one another, two dark blue ballpoints, one light blue ballpoint, one red ballpoint, one red that wasn't a ballpoint, and a pencil with its point facing in a different direction. Distraction. Where do I stop and you begin? It was time for a walk.

He left his apartment and headed for Ink, the stationery and card store where he bought his yellow legal pads. He kept a good stock of them on hand because he was always afraid he would run out of them and be doomed to continue his writing for the day on something plain and white. It would never feel the same.

Minutes later David Pond stopped in to the same card store that Martin Worthy had just walked out of. He had to get a birthday card for his aunt who had just turned eighty-three and a sympathy card for an associate whose sister-in-law had just turned forty and died in her sleep.

And much later on but still that same day Fiarette walked into the same card store and found a postcard that looked remarkably like David Pond. It was a reproduction of a pastel drawing of a man in a pink shirt wearing faded jeans and black boots. Both eyes were downcast and one hand was on his hip, the other one fingering the pockets. She bought the postcard and stuck it on her refrigerator door with a Mickey Mouse magnet.

CHAPTER TWENTY-ONE

There's nothing like a rainy day
that comes at the right time

Meanwhile, Kary was huffing and puffing with triumph. Steve moved in with her and so, it seemed, did everybody else. Kary said nothing; she tried to make it fun. And, in the beginning, it was. There would be a knock on the door and Steve would be there with a male friend, more male than friend. 'This is her,' he would say, smiling over at Kary, snug in the doorway, tugging her close, pecking her warmly on the lips. 'She smells like flowers,' Steve would tell his friend while his eyes stayed buckled on Kary. And someone might blush.

It was in those first weeks that she felt that whatever she did excited Steve, honestly thrilled him, made the rafters shake. She was encouraged to be herself. If she tied her hair in braids above her ears with a wildflower poking through, he made her think it was the most beautiful thing he had ever seen. They had each other's total attention. It was all about being royalty.

Sometimes he'd come home late, two, five, six or seven hours late, and say, 'I'm finally here. I guess you're mad.' And she'd say, hurting like hell. 'You're here. How can I be mad?' 'You're so pretty,' he'd say. And she'd let it go at that, the spotlight yet to be disfigured by the charade.

He brought home a friend he had met in the park, a guy who was waiting for some money from a lawyer for a bus accident he was in in St Croix. He sat up with Steve all night, complaining about recovering from some torn cartilege in his left knee and a broken right foot suffered in what he would only call 'an altercation'. At three o'clock in the morning he was still talking, this time about his escapades in Trinidad and the Trini rum he claimed could be found only in Trinidad and Brooklyn. Kary was the first to tire and she went off to sleep alone.

And then a few nights later Steve showed up with someone new. This one came in and played his guitar for the first half hour and the flute for the next half hour and a tape of a jam session for the next fifteen minutes. He called jazz 'yazz' and New Jersey 'New Yersey'. Again, Kary was the first to tire.

Then Steve came home with a guy in pink sunglasses who called the bathroom a 'washroom'.

And, finally, one night, six weeks into living together, Steve didn't come home at all. The next morning he showed up and said, 'I met this guy who's French and Puerto Rican. He's French from here to here,' he said, gesturing with the ledge of his hands from forehead to chin, 'and Puerto Rican where it counts.'

Kary blinked.

'And don't try to impress people with your sensitivity. It doesn't work for very long.'

Her tongue felt too big for her mouth. She listened to a voice she did not know in a room she did not want to be in, thinking. 'The best he ever treated me was at his brother's funeral.' Her role had come too easy.

'I wish you were less aware of yourself,' he said.

'Less aware of myself?' she asked.

'You always want to know where you are,' he said, 'just exactly where you are.'

And he walked out and Kary realized that she had been hurting since Sunday night. Sunday night he had gotten out of bed for a cigarette; when he had come back, instead of laying next to her, he put his head at the foot of their bed, his feet thick at her head. A spark of panic told her he would never be back in her bed: he was tired of it.

And she knew now that all the while he had been charming the pants off her, he had been charming the pain out of her, until he was good and ready to inflict the pain himself, the legendary pain of knowing another human being. And the pain of her beginnings—and more—was suddenly back. She understood the anguish of knowing that the very things she wanted were the ones she had always thrown away first.

Less than a month later she was telling Fiarette:

'When I stop being in love with someone, it's usually because they're not around anymore. People keep pulling disappearing acts on me.'

Fiarette wondered why she felt smugly happy at Kary's latest skirmish with Steve. She wanted to start humming 'Was that all it was? A night out on the town?' She wondered how she dared be so critical of her friend's romance while she herself was so sinfully frivolous: after all, she was starting to hear the word 'love' when she thought of David Pond. 'The object of my affection can change my complexion from white to rosy red,' she sang in her head.

'Kary, Kary, Kary, why can't you just let the attraction die a natural death? Get over it.'

'What about that guy at your office? Why don't you get over it?'

It was the kind of New York night where it would have been nice to eat outdoors; the air was heavy but you could talk yourself out of that and enjoy the stillness instead. Words didn't come easy; everything seemed overdone.

'Life is an idea, Kary, you never know what another person is up to. The world is full of smiling sinners.'

'I wish I had never learned the word "karma".'

Fiarette said nothing while Kary simply mused: 'I knew this girl at the last place I worked. She was the first virgin I've come across in a long time. She had been going out with this guy for three months but had never gone to bed with him. Can you imagine going out with someone for three months and not going to bed with him? I mean, what's the point. Like that girl in my office they call Long Tall Sally. The one whose mother won the Harvest Moon Ball doing the polka. She looks like a lemon lollipop with legs. She has a boyfriend and she doesn't even like sex.'

Fiarette felt a shadow cross her face. She hoped she wouldn't have to wait three months for David Pond. She wondered how to make the distance shorter. The sky looked swollen.

Kary kept going. 'She complained that he tried to pinch her ass a few times. Can you believe it? And then they got married and in six months they got divorced. The only furniture they had was a bedroom set. She got the four poster bed with the canopy and the night table and he got the triple dresser and the mirror. I thought how awful it was to break up a bedroom set. It seemed even worse than breaking up the marriage.'

Fiarette was going to ask what that had to do with karma, but she didn't.

'Fee, do you like me even when you're sick of me?'

'I like you but I can't take responsibility for you.'

'What about if I told you I was thinking of getting a gun?'

'For what?'

'For me.'

'Oh, don't be crazy. You wouldn't even know how to put the bullets in. You can't even put batteries in your camera right. And the only thing you know about your walkman is that when there's no red light it means it's off.'

'I'll practice. I'll test it.'

'How?' Where?'

'Down a toilet bowl.'

Kary ate nonfat yogurt and peaches for three days straight. She spent most of her time sitting in bed. That's where she was now. She had on white sweat socks with red tops and a rose pink nightgown that had looked sexy in Mays lingerie department. It was the day after a night when she had been too tired to wash her face but not tired enough to fall asleep. She turned the pages of a magazine and studied an ad for an Italian liqueur. An elegant looking man in a green silk dressing gown with strong orange piping was surveying a map of Piancavallo ski lifts, red lines for good skiers, black lines for advanced skiers. The copy: 'The whole point of life is to stay calm.'

She put on a purple t-shirt and red sweat pants and a string of beads she had saved from years ago from a New Orleans Mardi Gras parade. She wanted theatrics.

'What's that?' someone behind her said as they shared a corner waiting for a red light to go green.

'A rice cake,' she said. The first thing she noticed were his blue eyes, cold from too many goodbyes.

'Salty?'

'No, it's full of honey; it's sweet.'

'I've been walking behind you for a whole three blocks,' he told her, without smiling. His lips said, 'Where you from?' She felt her nipples go hard.

'New York City.'

'Great. I'm getting tired of New Yorkers who come from someplace else. They don't know what the city is all about so they read *New York* magazine so someone can tell them.'

His eyes seemed to stay open without blinking. She was already hoping he would ask her to go home with him. She was thinking that when the guys took her to wherever they lived instead of wanting to go back to her apartment, it made the whole event a real rock and roll dinosaur.

'I don't live too far from here. How about coming up for a beer?' He read her mind.

He stopped at a corner to talk to a black guy in green sweats with a blue felt cap tipped forward on his head.

On a burnt-out street in the East Village they walked through a downstairs locked door, through a building, into a courtyard, through the courtyard, to still another locked door and another building. In the middle of a block in New York City. They went up three flights of stairs to an apartment with a padlock on the door. Inside was a chill although it was a warm September day outside; no sun ever reached it. They sat on the floor on sisal mats because the only chair was missing some important parts. In one room was a bathtub and a tiny sink. There was a bathroom that was a toilet in a closet that you flushed by pulling a string weighted with a key. There was no stove.

'It costs one hundred dollars to live here,' he said, 'It's a real cold water flat.' The one light was a bulb on the ceiling. There was a copy of *Playguy* on a wooden table.

'Do you know what unanimous sex means?'

'No,' Kary said, 'I never heard of that.'

'It's when you'll do anything to me and you'll let me do anything to you.'

His eyes ate her up. She reached into her pocket wishing she could come up with some of the chocolate covered peanuts she had bought on Bleecker Street just before she had the rice cake.

She looked at the far wall. It was white pegboard with several diagrams in black outlining different kinds of tools: a hammer, pliers, a screwdriver. Each tool was placed where it belonged.

'Do you have hair on your legs?'

'I would if I didn't take it off.'

'I like hair on women's legs.'

He took her hand; his touch was bloodless.

'I like your hair,' he told her.

'Oh, good,' she smiled, 'I never know what to do with it.'

Her eyes were holes in her face, a face that reminded him of when he was a kid and he used to take a paper plate and punch two circles in it and slide it around his head with a rubber band and play spook.

She had no way of knowing he had committed homicide in Amsterdam, had a father who was a Nazi war criminal, had embezzled fifty thousand dollars from a leather shop in Brazil, had lived in Waco, Texas and read his horoscope every morning.

The first blow of the hammer was a downpour at close

range. She was in ruins but she hardly felt it. The moon was over and the curtain was down. And she had been wondering what had happened to that beer he had asked her up for.

CHAPTER TWENTY-TWO

Bacall and Bogey were 20 and 45
when they were married in 1945.

You say prayers for the people you love and Fiarette had prayed many a prayer for Kary. She loved her friend. Kary had reminded her of the special richness of knowing someone for a long time. Now she was full of memories. Heavy shoes. There would be no more new memories. She was pained by the urgency of something being over. What good times she had were all she would ever have. Kary, the astonished heart, whose all time favorite book was *The Great Gatsby*; whose all time favorite movie was *A Place in the Sun*. Kary who proclaimed that Nexus Botanoil was the only shampoo to use. Kary who would say, 'I hope I never get grey hair—it's not even a color.'

Fiarette lit the last stick of sweet nut incense that she had brought when she and Kary spent a rainy January week in Nassau. Fiarette's thoughts were humble strings that could not make music. It only worked when she allowed herself to call life a technical memory and shut down her emotions to things like the wrapping around the incense. 'Incense is mentioned in the scriptures. It is a good omen. Some people burn it for luck, others for love. These sticks will leave a beautiful smell for a very long time.'

Kary, who had called a black guy she went out with 'a burnt muppet'. Kary, who had taught Fiarette the trick of stuffing cotton balls between your toes when you were putting toenail polish on so the polish went on the nails and not on the toes.

Kary: they went to Europe together, both for the first time, and got t-shirts at a disco in London called Sundown and met some English guy at Russell Square who told them 'Red skies in the morning...' They went to Nassau and met Garth and Kevin from Memphis and stayed up all night drinking ginger beer. And then out to Johnny and Sam's boat where they stayed up all night drinking gin and coconut water. And the Mississippi Bar in Pointe-a-Pitre in Guadaloupe where they stayed up all night with Philippe from Havana and Jacques from Toronto drinking rum and pineapple juice.

Kary: they saw *Cabaret* together. And Buckingham Palace. And places that had no names but would be remembered forever anyway.

Kary was gone and Fiarette knew she had something to do with it.

She wished she could talk about it to someone. She wished it could be David Pond. The thought made her smile. He would be part of her life; she suddenly felt strangely sure of it. But, like Alex, like Kary, he too might not last forever. This time she would try to remember that love only pretends to have ambitions. Love, a street fighting man wiped out by deception. The world was full of configurations in need of nourishment. Unhappiness was the consequence of inaction. Things would happen—she was sure of it; when their time had come, things would happen. Her mood changed;

suddenly, she no longer felt impoverished.

Before she could even get a smile out, her mood changed back; quickly the city was littered; she became despondent, she went dead. She knew she would get to a point in her life where nobody would be left—not a mother, not a father, not a spot of her own blood anywhere, not a lover, not a rare friend. She would search the streets for someone she knew and no one would remember where she had been last year. She wouldn't know how to begin. She would get old and not be able to travel as far as a whisper. All she would want would be a quiet country path to ride a bike on but she wouldn't know how to get there.

Kary was gone and Fiarette knew over and over she had something to do with it. The thought haunted her. Remorse is the curse of getting older. She would live alone and have no one to say goodnight to.

CHAPTER TWENTY-THREE

Men who move furniture
are known as facility planners

David Pond had breakfast at Arby's that morning. He had a wrinkled newspaper under his arms folded in four at the financial page. He had the breakfast special, a ham and egg sandwich and regular coffee for one eighteen with tax. It was the best breakfast deal around. Every morning they gave you a cash register receipt that showed the time you ordered breakfast. Today's said 3 October 9.17 a.m. The recorded accuracy appealed to him. He was a lawyer.

He sat across from a man who looked like a writer, scratching away on a yellow legal pad. The man drank coffee, black, and asked David Pond if he wanted an extra Half and Half for his coffee because the countergirl had given him one by mistake.

That night Martin Worthy sat in his apartment. The night table by his bed held a yellow legal pad, a green plastic pencil sharpener the size of a thumbnail, and a brown ceramic ashtray. A paperback copy of *Last Tango in Paris* had a red leather bookmark at page 35. He opened it and read: 'I wanted to clean up,' the man said, 'but the police wouldn't let me. They didn't believe in suicide; too much blood all over.' A copy of Agatha

Christie's *Peril at End House*. Three weeks of the *New Yorker*. A story on Jack Kerouac from the *Sunday Times* magazine a month ago.

Martin Worthy understood that a plan for living was the only way to get by. A plan meant an understanding of time while you were facing an audience. It was no easy achievement in real life, a scrambled holiday, where people spent more time searching out new formulas than living them. He became strangely afraid of his writing, a world within a world, where he could feel the words running into pages, where his ego framed in roses was being enhanced as never before, because he could control. He gave other people's lives an elastic lust for all things, living and haunting, while he, and not they, could revise and rewrite, scatter their dreams off a roof or into the arms of a mad stranger and end them forever. He could land them in jail or land them in hell; he alone was the rough inspiration.

He sat there thinking about his characters coming into shape as the pencil went round the paper. They began in darkness. He wondered just how much he had to tell about each character; some seemed so much more talkative than others. Some were grimy and some were candles. Should he account for everything they did—their mornings, where they had breakfast, what their beds smelled like, how many times they brushed their teeth? He did not always see their faces so clearly, but he could always see the way they moved, the cut of their hair and the color of their pain.

What of where they came from? Some had no home town and lived on frayed limits. They were not shaped by immediate environment. They were companions to oblivion, serene and steep. Still others clearly came from a yesterday and that yesterday came with them, controlling the damage and diminishing the mourning. Some were guilty of one cast of sin but were not likely to commit another. The woman who coveted her neighbor's husband might never steal a dime. They didn't always look where they were going; they spoke of dreams weary of waiting. Whatever they were they seemed to come that way.

There were days he didn't write a thing. It wasn't that he wouldn't, but that he couldn't. He sat and only made the periods on the page darker by pushing his pencil point into and around them; he got mad, but they never came, these people; they were out playing out of his grasp, past his reach. Then they would be back. Crisp details. He could barely contain his glee. He was triumphant. Complete.

He was scissoring the pages having to do with the character in his book whose journey was shadowed by imperfect joys. One minute they were people; then they were camouflaged by instant obscurity, dead as a fallen balloon. He knew how to say no to them. Reality was disturbing but it remained his favorite canvas.

He could not plan his writing too far ahead and yet he knew when the time was right. More and more he felt like a writer.

In the downstairs hallway of his building someone had left last month's *National Enquirer*. He had picked it up. There was an article about love.

Q. What percentage of love affairs end up on the rocks?
A. A surprise seventy percent of romantic relationships do not last for the twenty- to thirty-year-old age group.

Even in his book he had watched two such relationships come to an end.

He had begun to understand and to respect both the needs and the foibles of the writer. He found it made life easier if he took a red pencil and drew two parallel lines at the end of a chapter; it gave him a sense of structure. It reminded him that what happened had happened and to go on from there.

He had never thought himself a fastidious man; he never cared about the hint of blue in a shirt, only in a sky. But now he was experiencing a reverence for the quality of a piece of paper: he refused even to jot a note to the mailman on anything but a square sheet of thick handsome paper that felt like it had been sliced right off a tree. He loved yellow legal pads and wished that he could figure out a way to get them for free. He discovered too that not all yellow legal pads were the same. Some were too shiny and made the side of his hand slide around. And some were full of rag and just right. Flimsy typing paper hurt his feelings. You could see through it, but, worse, when you held a sheet in your hands, you could feel that you could see through it. He soon realized he couldn't use it even to write a note to himself.

When he had assembled several sheets relating to one character, he would label them on a mint green four by five sheet of memo paper and keep them together with a big red paperclip. The red paperclip tagged personalities that needed finishing. He used red paperclips on everything he wrote that was waiting for something else to happen. He used everyday skinny silver paperclips for household records, income tax returns, Con Ed bills. Red paperclips seemed right for his people; he wanted them to brim with life and feelings, with insubordinations, with thick pleasantries, with spirited wrinkles, with the deterioration of reason. He wanted to devour them with feelings, feelings that escalated and then fell to earth, gripping but getting dusty; there must be excess; excess could breathe abundance because life could so quickly be spirited away and become muffled and sober. He wanted to overdo to make up for the parts that lay gloomy.

He understood the idea was to get the story down and the rest would feed itself. The important thing was chewing very, very well. He learned how to pay attention to details. Details happened when you looked. How big things are, how long they last, how they change color, how people change places, how night takes place, how the street sounds after an ambulance has raced through it, empty containers.

I am a realist, he told himself over and over. I want to mirror contemporary life to the soap opera extreme. I want to catalogue today. Everything seems relevant, the moving targets and the fractured songs. It is important to know what is happening because what is happening is change. I want the exquisite detail of accuracy when all else is a lie. I want the passionate specifics that evidence tomorrow.

Yes, he wanted honesty. People want heroes but heroes are fantasies. He wanted the good guys to get gunned down and the bad guys to get away with things—that was the way life happened. That was the thwarted way things scrambled into focus. Somewhere down the line it all balanced out. There were rewards and lollipops; yet it was all genuinely sinister. For him books and movies and cartoons were as much a brave new world as the real thing.

CHAPTER TWENTY-FOUR

G. K. Chesterton once said of Times Square at night
that a person who couldn't read
might think it paradise.

David Pond brought his wife flowers Wednesday night, purple flowers that looked like they were made out of folded tissue paper that had been teased. The next day she looked at them and knew he had given them to her as a substitute for communication. He could not soothe her. He could not soothe himself. Some new margin of grief was there.

Some relationships you fall into and others you struggle against. There remains a sad reality to the ones you struggle against. They had never talked enough, David and her; she had tried, she was always trying to catch his words until she began to worry that too much talking takes the mystery away, that if love is too predictable it can lose its heat. She tried to talk him out of loving her in the early days, needing him to reject her; rejection was her theory of value. But he never caught on; he kept right on telling her he loved her, over and over, until she would wonder who he was trying to convince.

Every Tuesday morning she would see her therapist on the eighth floor of a grand old building on the West Side that had wood elevator walls where someone had scratched:

Ann likes dick
Ann sucks dick
Ann fucks anything

And then someone else had scratched

Who is Ann?

She wondered if Ann, whoever she was, was happy; she wondered if she had considered therapy. She wondered if maybe Ann went to the same therapist she went to and had scratched these messages on the elevator walls herself.

That Tuesday morning she went into the waiting room and studied the black rectangular table; in the far left corner of it was a black vase and in the far right corner was a glass candy dish; in the other left corner was a piece of grey pottery with an orange stripe; and in the other corner was a ruby paperweight. Precisely in the center was a long oblong glass dish that looked like it should be full of celery and carrot slices. Her therapist had told her just last week that the need to rearrange something was a sign of inner chaos. She wanted desperately to rearrange that table.

Her therapy sessions would go something like this:

'How are things in bed?'

'Fine,' she would say, thinking she would like a piece of the candy that was always in a little dish on the table to her right; every week the variety of candy changed, aqua mints, nibs of licorice, lemon sours, and she wondered if patients ate it or if the therapist changed it.

'Are you sure about that?'

She wanted to be honest with her indecision. 'Sometimes, sometimes I just lay there and don't feel a thing.'

'How often is that?'

'Oh,' and she would hesitate, wanting to get it just right, 'maybe one in four . . . no, one in three times.'

'Mmmm,' her therapist would say.

And she would wonder if 'mmmm' meant normal, the fringe of normal, or not nearly normal enough, but she did not know how to ask, and she was not at all sure answers could ever be found.

'Sometimes I'm sure he's thinking of someone else when he's making love to me.'

'The possibility exists that you introduce jealousy into the relationship to stir up some excitement.'

Other things her therapist would say were: 'You let yourself suffer too much for other people's failures.' Mrs David Pond thought that one over, cradled it on the curve, but decided that was nothing at all like her. She smiled an unyielding smile and longed for a cup of strong coffee, very strong and very sweet.

She had no way of knowing that at that moment a girl at a word processing machine in her husband's law office was fantasizing, staring at a blank screen. 'I want to go to bed with David Pond.' Fiarette. Fiarette and her extravagant passions. Mrs David Pond had no way of knowing about Fiarette and the strength of custom made mavericks. She was a clenched fist who had no way of knowing about Fiarette.

The thunder came in short spurts that hot autumn day, snapping like firecrackers across a hand made heaven. The sun broke out and the noise was hot.

Fiarette and Mrs David Pond both heard the same thunder. It was loud and made them jump.

Mrs David Pond's thinking was soothing and measured; it was time to start getting him over him. Fiarette was thinking just the opposite. Fiarette was thinking how his voice stayed in her head even though most of the time she heard it, he was talking to someone else. She was so full of him. Their eyes met more and more lately; more and more and more they were in the same place at the same time.

At work Fiarette was reading *Points to Remember. Optional Statistical Applications.* 'If numbers with decimals vary in length, three tab settings per column are needed.' She didn't understand what that meant. But she figured she'd better learn in case David Pond needed decimals typed some day.

The thunder stopped. Mrs David Pond wondered if it was a mistake to confront your husband about irrational fears. She did not want to tell her husband (nor her therapist) that she was seriously considering the 'non-surgical face lift,' a series of treatments that worked by an isometric principle, an anti-gravity machine that delivered low frequency energy to correct sagging skin. She wondered how much more her face might sag; it scared her to see it happen, to be forced to see the resilient strength of distance.

Sometimes her therapist got her mad, like when she said, 'Where did you learn not to trust men?' It sounded like a dreadful deficiency and she had never thought of it that way at all. Had she learned not to trust men? Had she read the wrong books?

That life could make some sense, have at least an occasional night with a bright yellow moon, could mean pattern, could be a river that ran not smooth, not pretty, but in one direction, was what she yearned for.

One day at work David Pond walked into the typing pool and brought with him a sixteen page handwritten memo to be typed. Fiarette looked at it and realized she loved a man who had an absolutely indecent

handwriting. 'His 'dear' looked like 'dim'. He handed
the document over to her and said, 'If you can't read my
handwriting, just come in and ask.' So, Fiarette tried
hardly at all to decode even the most mildly distorted
scrawls. More than once that afternoon she went into his
office. The first time he was on the telephone and looked
up at her; his eyes got dressed up and he never once
looked away from her while he kept right on talking on
the phone. She felt dizzy between her legs. She wanted
to be able to unbutton that starched pink shirt of his.
She wondered if his skin was hot or cool. She wondered
how his fingers would feel inside her. She wanted to lick
his nipples. She wanted to nuzzle his underwear and
make it all wet.

The third time she went into his office that afternoon
she was pretty sure he knew what she was up to. She felt
like someone sure to swivel to victory. But how would
she finally get there. In the next few days she considered
just coming right out and propositioning him and then
she began to worry about what kind of things might
make him say no. She had read an article that asked
'What stops you from really expressing your sexuality?'
The list:

> an unwanted pregnancy
> feeling guilty
> social disapproval
> religious or moral reasons
> fear of disease
> lack of desire
> fear of being inadequate.

All of them might be applicable here and the situation
seemed to get more bleak as the list went on. She

thought, my God, there are more reasons to say no than to say yes.

The article continued with the next question: 'What is the best way of saying no?' She didn't want to hear about it; she hoped it would never come to that. She wanted to stay positive in a world where Max Headroom is a star.

And she began waking up with David Pond on her mind—he started every day, a homemade halo. She began to wake up before the alarm told her to. She began to long to see him. He walked into the office about seventeen minutes to ten every morning, but hours before that, still in bed, eyes just opening, his face began to take place in her head, the eyes first, or sometimes his bottom lip, the left side, the side that started to curl into the most knowing of smiles the last few times they had passed each other in the hall. He always looked like he was about to say something but he never did; he just locked his eyes and grinned, which was far more haunting than either the spoken or the written word.

A day later she was going up on the up escalator and he was going down. They gazed and their eyes stayed put all the way of his down and her up. And it didn't end there. Ignoring the steady struggle of people on their own ups and downs, she moved slightly to the right and he moved a little to the left and they kept right on looking at each other.

That night Fiarette wondered why the spirit of trashy sex always made her feel like a goddess, made her feel a brush with fame—why she liked the idea of being the woman men thought of when they were making love to somebody else.

She found herself playing with words at work thinking of how to get her message across: 'I know it is dangerous to put things in writing, especially sexual advances.' She crossed out 'sexual advances' and changed it to 'stuff like this'. And continued. 'But I have never been much of a talker—the words bubble up inside my head but die before they reach my tongue. So I decided to make my move on paper.' She crossed out everything after 'stuff like this' and then decided she didn't like the word 'stuff' but couldn't think of anything better.

Later on she tried: 'I know this is in direct and shameful violation of our firm's sexual harassment policy, but I think you're very sexy.' No.

or

'I think you're hot.' Maybe.

or

'I'd like to have a drink with you.' No, she just couldn't be that forward.

Maybe she should wait until after the first of the year when she could write, 'I just got a nice raise. How about letting me buy you a drink?'

Or 'There's something about you that excites the hell out of me. Would you like to have a drink some night?' That sounded a bit too seductive and soon became 'Do you think we could have a drink some night?' which had the right tone—slightly submissive and very out-of-breath—but still wasn't quite it. Maybe just 'There's something about you that . . . .' and leave a bunch of dots. Or maybe exclamation points would be better than dots—one was sultry, the other wicked, but adolescent.

She didn't like any of them. She was after the acceptable combination of humor and heat. Whatever she decided on, though, she was sure she would add something she had seen in a porn ad in the *Voice*, 'Discretion assured.' She would place it over to the bottom left like an R.S.V.P.

The following Thursday it fell into place with a simple note that said it all.

'I think you're sexy. Do with this sentiment what you will.'

She was very nervous while she wrote it; the first time she wrote 'statement' instead of 'sentiment' and had to start all over again.

She put the note—the few words standing alone on a sheet of yellow legal paper—into a 9 x 13 interoffice envelope and walked it into David's office, wanting to hang around until he opened it, but managing only a 'this is from me' and walking out.

That night she lay in bed with extra cream on her face and hoped he was thinking of her while he was fucking his wife. Fiarette assumed all married people made love every chance they got; why not celebrate the neighborhood? She would say to him when the time was right: 'I want you to know I don't make a hobby of writing notes like that. I just try hard never to be ashamed of my feelings. It keeps me sane, it keeps me honest.' Something like that. She hoped this interpretation would remedy any defiant strategies she might be forced to use.

The next few days Fiarette got high at lunch on a dime bag. She wondered what he would think if she suddenly appeared at the door to his office and said something like, 'You know, I think you're hot stuff.'

And Mrs David Pond was at her therapist's:

'It gets me mad that he can be happy without me.'

'But you can be happy without him. Why don't you try that?'

Mrs David Pond could feel the tension. 'That makes me feel spiteful.' Her teeth were clenched and her voice snapped.

'It must come naturally, any separation,' the therapist told her. 'Find yourself, allow yourself to find more of yourself, and you will enjoy him more. Let him be.'

For a moment it sounded clever with dignity, but the expert witness in her was overwhelmed with the idea of letting him go and believing he would come back.

CHAPTER TWENTY-FIVE

Bela Lugosi was buried in his Dracula cape

Mrs David Pond woke up to a sad sky that morning and the only thing that fit in was doing the laundry. The laundermat was crowded but not too crowded. She waited for the woman with the blonde baby in the stroller to pull her clothes out of the washer and then she threw hers in. She had two other washers going but none of it felt harmonious; she hated the drying, washing and folding. She smiled at the baby and the baby smiled back. The baby had two cookies, one in each hand; the mother smiled at her, straight haired, face round but glowing. She felt terribly upset by everything and was glad when the laundry was done and she could get out of there.

And on her way to the laundermat later that same day, Fiarette saw Margie the old lady. She could tell by the way the old woman slowed her pace that she had something to say; it was, of course, about her late husband.

'He never comforted me,' she began, looking straight into Fiarette's eyes, 'but he allowed me to comfort him.'

Fiarette wanted to know, 'What do you do when you get in a bad mood?'

But the old lady simply said, 'When you live alone, you always think you smell something burning.' She waited a few moments and went on. 'I was mad at him because he was living in my house. I missed it being no more my house. It was the only house I had ever loved and I had lived in many. But as with all things I have loved the love confounded me and finally had to be surrendered.'

While her wash was soaking, Fiarette picked up a copy of *Esquire*. It said that at age twenty men have one hundred and four orgasms a year, forty-nine of them solo. They wake up six mornings per month with erections. And the angle of erection is ten percent above horizontal. She wondered about David; how many orgasms did he have with his wife? She made some fast calculations and wished he was sixty years old; then, if the magazine was right, he would be having only thirty-five orgasms a year, four of them solo, and she wouldn't have to worry so much.

David Pond, as a matter of fact, was reading the very same issue, but he had started with the cover story. It began with an illustration of the profiles of a woman and a man: 'But I can't resist you,' said one. 'Me, neither,' said the other. It was entitled: 'Do you really want to have an affair?'

Neither Fiarette nor David, though, happened to see a flyer pinned up at the supermarket early in the week advertising a Sunday afternoon lecture about 'Cheating: The Modern Epidemic.' It promised to explore motivations and maneuvers and to let all parties feel like they were rightful owners in the triangle.

CHAPTER TWENTY-SIX

Tolstoy observed that the ability to blush
is a sign a person can love.

The firm's thirty-fifth anniversary party was a day away. Only legal and nonlegal staff were invited, which made it sound like everybody, while specifically excluding wives and husbands. Fiarette had no intention of going because she knew if David was there she would get drunk on wine and, bleak with majesty and passion, she would do exactly what she knew she shouldn't. See your travel agent for full details, but there would most definitely be a break in the weather. She had no intention of going but she found herself there just the same, in one of those ballrooms just off the gracious lobby in an East Side hotel.

Their eyes met and she felt like a desperado. Suddenly they were dancing and she was so excited at how close they were that she started to see double. Life told the best stories. She smelled his neck and shoulder and swallowed hard.

'I'm not sexy,' he picked that moment to whisper to her. Well, at least he had read the note.

'You are to me.' Her voice was so low she wondered where it had come from, how the words could have happened. And she felt that slight but unmistakable moist spot between her legs, secrets locked in curls.

'How close do you think we can dance before people start talking,' she asked him, so close they were almost there.

'I think they're already talking.'

And they found two soft seats away from the music where she had two more Black Russians. Then she told him, 'Do you know I have a postcard at home that looks just like you? I found it at a card shop. It's a guy in jeans with an apricot shirt, one arm at his side, the other one curled at his hip, head down, and I swear it looks just like you.' He sort of smiled. She kept talking. 'I once worked with a girl who had a life-threatening crush on a guy she worked with. One night he followed her into the down elevator and kissed her. She said the only reason she said no when he asked her to go home with him was because she had on torn underwear.' Intermediate pause. 'That would never stop me.' Pause. 'I want to make love to you as soon as possible.'

And David Pond blushed.

And Fiarette danced with other people that night, but he didn't dance anymore at all.

On her birthday, Mrs David Pond's husband gave her a humming bird with a red underbelly.

'This is delicate and beautiful just like you are,' he told her, with a careful smile.

She smiled back, thinking. You were thinking of someone delicate and beautiful when you bought it, but it wasn't me.

And she was, of course, right.

She placed the humming bird on a shelf in the china closet and knew she would never stop suffering the blues, dark echoes and the surrender of acceptance.

She lay in her bed in the middle of the next afternoon. She thought of how her mother always used to be whistling; never a tune, just dabs of notes, specks with no apparent connection. She would always stare straight ahead of her while she whistled, off into north of July, a space no one else could see. She had grown up knowing that her mother whistled because it somehow made her feel less lonely. Now she was so lonely herself that she began to miss furniture—furniture she hadn't seen in a lifetime, the highly-polished wardrobe in her parents' bedroom when she was a child. They called it a chifforobe, a word she never heard used again for the rest of her life; now she wondered if she had heard right. When her father was away at work, she would open the door and touch his ties, marvelous tiny designs of maroons, rich browns and blues that seemed to shine. She missed the curved glass china cabinet in their dining room and the folding wooden tray table with the hand painted snow scene that she would eat from when she watched 'Howdy Doody' or 'Lights Out' or 'The Milton Berle Show'. She missed the *New York Post* which was called *The Bronx Home News*.

She remembered how she had gone through a period hoping David's mother would die because he was always so feverishly close to her, writing her letters all the time, sending her dried fruit from Lord and Taylor, watching her money market funds for her. She remembered how she had hoped David's cat would die, too; she was so jealous of that cat. She had never understood how to deal with that loneliness and the jealous rage that came later. Everything was a disappointing conclusion, a narrow crime. She remembered how she had dealt with that paralyzing loneliness as a child: she kept dozens of marbles in a tough paper bag and she would spill them in a rush over the wooden floor; their sound was startled luxury. She was less than five.

I was always shy as a child, she was thinking, but she wasn't a child anymore. She was at a distance of one note from life. What name could she give this feeling that continued to keep her apart? What was fun for others was frightening to her. It was hard sometimes even to feel relaxed with David, to feel adequate, to feel the pure and simple freedom of taking her shoes off, of slipping her bra off, for God's sake, and feeling comfortable doing these things in the company of another person. She had never felt as comfortable with another person as she felt when she was all alone, not with her mother, not with her father, never in school, not with a teacher, not with a friend.

Being shy had never been sophisticated poetry; it was more like she had lost her footing. Would the words come out right, she always wondered. Would she be funny when it was time to be funny and sober when it was time to be straight? Would she drink too much or not enough? Could people guess that she longed simply to lose herself? Where had it all begun, the fatigue of exploring her identity?

Nothing would make Mrs David Pond happy unless all the women of the world suddenly became five feet two, one hundred and fifty pounds, and wrinkled.

How she wanted to be sexy and say to her husband 'make love to me'—but she could not. She wanted to rub her cunt in his face like they did in the paperback novels but she wanted him to ask her first. So, she sat back, and enjoyed the brillant function of pain.

Mrs David Pond wondered if she would ever be able to watch *The Last Picture Show* and see Cybille Shepard and not mourn her own lost youth, the days when wrinkles happened to other people and she couldn't imagine decay around her eyes.

The wastebasket in Mrs David Pond's room that night had empty packages, wrappers of Nutribel nourishing hydrating emulsion and Ritz Revenescence. She had spent hours walking through Macy's and Lord and Taylor's hoping for someone to sell her a cream that would make her look young again. She did not like what she saw in the mirror and she knew that her husband must see it, too. When the gloom fell over his face, she understood that he was aging, too. But her aging was rapid, the authority of a brazen power, the disgrace of collapse. She was sure David saw the day by day shading but was kind enough for peaceful indifference. She was sure he was trying to get away from her. She was weary of the disappointment of solitude with gels and bases, ready to cancel the adventure, to murder her mind.

She dreamed that night that she and David were on a cruise: there were rows of chairs on the top deck and she sat down in one and said, 'Look, the ocean starts all over again in the middle.' And he said it only looked like that because of the angle of the ship.

CHAPTER TWENTY-SEVEN

Gorky's Little Girls Called his Paintings 'Broken Toys'

While Mrs David Pond was thinking how hard it was to be forty-one when everyone else was seventeen, Martin Worthy was understanding all over again what it felt like to be a writer. An explosion of personalities found its way on to paper. Sometimes it was worthless racket, but always with an urgency of poetics, as much frantic as fiction. He wondered what could be done to characters who have outlived their usefulness, failed to fulfil the rumored promise of love, turning out instead to be like every other dream that plagued man, a humble enterprise ending with a burst of rage. What does a writer do with these people as they struggle for dignity in vast, humming streets? How honest should they be with themselves and with others? How far should they run for safety and how long should it take them to get there?

He remembered his wife and the summer of that black bathing suit and how he had told her all summer long how much he loved her cleavage. He wondered how many times he had made love to one woman and thought of another. He wasn't sure if it was more or less than the average man. He wondered what he could call his story now that it was close to reality. HOTEL BLUE he would call it, life seen as a batch of rooms dying against the line of the night. He would design a bookcover for it. He worried that sometimes the writing was not passionate enough; it was taking his characters too long to make up their minds. Were they fallen leaders, feeble faucets? He understood for the first time how hard it was for people to take care of themselves as they struggled with the damp cheering. The only defiance some of them knew was grabbing a bottle from mama.

He started a new folder now and called it STILL TO COME. Characters who tangled for more music with less distortion.

He wanted more than dialogue; he wanted memorable lines, scene stealers, heartbreakers. Lines that were full of eyes. His words had to do something, like move mountains and shine for the Lord.

The next morning Martin Worthy got a copy of *The Cradle of Soaring Cemetery News* in his mailbox. Call your favorite counselor, one heading prompted, a selection of indoor and outdoor crypt spaces at substantial pre-construction discounts will be available on a pre-need basis. It is wise to purchase now and save as much as forty per cent. He wondered what the married man in his story would do if his wife died suddenly, unexpectedly. Where would he bury her? Do people in novels think of things like cemetery plots? What kind of people think of things like cemetery plots?

It was late October. The cemetery offered a fall foliage walk that would meet at two p.m. at the south gate; it called itself the most 'viable' cemetery in the area.

Then in one corner of the last page there was a joke column:

One woman to another as they leave the supermarket. 'I've always wanted to spend money lavishly, but I certainly never thought it would be on sugar, milk and bread.'

The title of the joke column was "Dig This".

CHAPTER TWENTY-EIGHT

'I've been betrayed so often by tomorrows
that I don't dare promise them.'
Bette Davis to Franchot Tone in 'Dangerous'

Fiarette was trying to come up with reasons why she
shouldn't see him. She tried to tell herself she didn't
need him but she knew she would be devastated if
David Pond didn't want her. While she longed for a
Sunday that had a life of its own, Sunday had become
just a day that was one day closer to him. She wanted
less time with her brain and more time with her body.
She was obsessed with him, saw him everywhere,
images on a street of dreams. She indulged herself in the
mythical capacity of love.

Mrs David Pond was thinking how love had never
been a happy occasion. It was just one of those things
that goes without saying. A crowded repetition of what
she could never manage to leave behind.

Mrs David Pond was thinking how *Penny Serenade*
with Cary Grant had been her mother's favorite movie;
the two of them had spent years waiting for it to be on
t.v. Now it was on television all the time and her mother
was dead. She had needed her something awful. Her
mother's attention had been vital to her obsessive need
for esteem. Her mother was her daytime drama. Just the
week before her mother had died she had reassured her

daughter that she was not going bald just because a grey
streak that she had been dying brown for ten years was
getting thinner and thinner. She missed her mother very
much but she missed her most of all when she was
invaded by emotional pain; at those sorrowful moments
she understood her mother's own anguish and how little
she had done to soften it. Her mother died from a gas
leak; slowly and steadily it came from the remains of an
old ceiling gas light fixture that had never been properly
capped in the hundred-year-old tenement she lived in.
She suspected the leak for years but insisted she never
believed it was really dangerous. Now she wondered if
her mother had wanted to die the way she did.

Mrs David Pond wished she could have known how to
be sexy, how to play with sinister promise and warm
protection. Maybe she should have dipped her nipple
into his mouth when he least expected it, and they might
have huddled in glory. She spent her days looking at old
people on the subways and in the parks trying to guess
their ages, wondering how she would age, how she
would look as her skin slipped and shriveled.

And she thought of her father. The last time she had
seen him alive, he was sitting in the kitchen with a glass
of gin playing 'Red River Valley' on his harmonica. He
wore the white pants from an elegant gabardine suit he
had worn some forty years before. She knew now that
her biggest lies had always been about her father. He
was full of jokes about niggers and jews and it had made
her sick. She remembered when her father smashed the
dishes that belonged to the Orthodox Jews who rented
the bottom floor of their house. The dishes, all shapes
and all sizes, were kept in the basement of the house in
the Bronx, stacked and covered on narrow shelves on
pieces of oilcloth. One day for a reason she never knew

he got angry and threw all the dishes on the basement floor. She didn't see it happen. She didn't know if he threw them down or if he had yanked the oilcloth and sent them all crashing to the floor. She knew only that there wasn't one dish left. It made her sob but the next day he took her to see an Esther Williams movie at Radio City Music Hall.

She remembered family picnics, twenty-five and thirty years ago, how all the women in the family had a specialty dish, the honey cakes and the cheddar cheese pies. The words 'cancer' and 'bypass surgery' never came up—everyone was too young, wild-eyed with optimism, too pleased with life to talk about being sick. Everyone got to sit in orchestra seats. She remembered the bingo cards—how every holiday the whole family played bingo and how everyone had a few lucky cards. They would be marked on the back: 'This is Margaret's card. Christmas Day, 1956. Keep your hands off!' Everything was so reasonable. Now the city was in a different mood.

She remembered her father's dying days, the shivers of wartime, when he had to get on the bus every day to go to the hospital for chemotherapy treatments. But he did not have the money for a taxi and they never had a car, and she remembered how painful it was for him to get together the energy for those journeys. That was when she first understood that death is merciful, but dying is not.

She thought of her own littered marriage and how she lied right from the start. How she would write to David's mother and say things like 'David and I are closer all the time' because she knew that was what the mother wanted to hear.

She was no good at comforting others and now the

chance was gone. There had been a time when something very simple could make her happy—like a peach.

The Kleenex was no good—it was in shreds. The tears had turned to sobs and she heard herself talking to God. Did I ask for too much? She longed to know. I need so little. I needed only to feel necessary. She sat naked with her legs spread, not for any reason, only because it felt better. The window was open but there was no air, only the sound of steam. It was late afternoon and the lamp on her night table was on; she looked at her shadow in the quilt. Everything cast a shadow. She forgot what she looked like and remembered only that she wanted to feel loved. And she knew that she would die because there was no love. She started thinking about the things she owned and who would find what and who, if anyone, would linger over them, the papers about cosmetic surgery, the handkerchiefs with crocheted edges her mother had given her, the leather photograph album where she looked happy until she was three and her sister was born, the silver bracelet, the pink crystal heart on the gold chain that broke and never got fixed. 'I have neither the stamina nor the interest.'

She looked at the drug company's warnings that came with her prescription for the antidepressants. There were headings like 'Description,' 'Clinical Pharmacology,' 'Contraindications,' and, finally, 'Dosage and Administration.' She smiled at the thought of getting caught red-handed. She decided the rest of the bottle ought to do it.

And then she decided to get some sleep.

David Pond was sitting at his desk reading the firm's newsletter. He liked to do the puzzles. This month's were all about 'mothers.' Who was Mother Shipton?

Who was Ma Ferguson? Who was the Mother of Minerva? What is a Mother Hubbard? Then there was another quiz about songs: 'Here's the line, what's the title?'

'Keep away from bootleg hootch.'

'Undimmed by human tears.'

'I know how it feels to have wings on your heels.'

He felt the rumblings of a smile that went from ear to ear and his eyes felt too big for his face. He didn't know what had happened but a remarkable clarity told him it was time for his marriage to be over. There hadn't been many women in his life; there never had been time. He lived on obscure information. He wondered if most things came to an indifferent end. He didn't think he would hurt one bit when he left her. He wondered if the girl with the red hair could make him know how it feels to have wings on his heels. He knew his wife could not. He knew there was no easy way to tell a woman who happens to be your wife that you no longer love her. Love never stayed the same, he decided; either it grew stronger or it disfigured itself. Love made life beautiful, he knew that, but love now meant something it hadn't seemed to mean before. Now he needed someone to make him feel young, to put wings on his heels. He felt no obligation anywhere else.

That was what he was thinking all the way home that night right up until he turned the key in the lock only to walk in and find she was dead; the ex-object of his affections. Dead.

CHAPTER TWENTY-NINE

Do men today really have more style?
Or just more styling options?
From an ad by Gillette for the Dry Look collection

The law firm had announced the death of Mrs David Pond with nothing more than a few lines under a heading entitled 'Personal'. It was the same heading that was used if someone found an earring in the ladies' room or if their ham sandwich was stolen from the refrigerator in the lunch room. That was a little over three weeks ago, and Fiarette's passion for David Pond had grown hotter, shamefully hotter, lamentably hotter, the lament for the well-sprung bed.

She got high at a late lunch all alone one day and came back early and stopped by his office, that little office in a long line of little offices along the northeast corridor. Everything was decided according to how many years you were out of law school, whether you had a window, the size of your window, the size of your closet, the mold of your chair, how many pictures were allowed on your wall, which wall, and who chose the pictures, and the wall they got to go on. 'If I take a day off from work and call you some afternoon from my bedroom and ask you to take a long break and hop in a taxi and come visit me, would you?' She knew she was purring.

'If I can get away,' oh, so straight and still blushing.

Fiarette wanted an unconditional promise that not only would he come but he couldn't wait to get there. She wanted to make him forget the murky steps of being a lawyer.

'Let me tell you about my apartment. You can see the top of the Empire State Building from my bedroom.'

He smiled but left it there.

'We wouldn't be doing anything wrong now. I mean it's not like you're still married. It's not like you can do anything to hurt her now. What could possibly make it wrong?' She tried to remember all those reasons in the magazine why someone might say no to an affair. She wondered what kind of reasons he could come up with.

David Pond was losing track of himself. Work was starting to frighten him, to overrule him. He was part of the star struck demons on a crusade suffering the hardships of contending. But the practice of law was a faint exercise that no longer stretched his ego. That was where his career had failed—it had been a digression that was now a distraction.

'Why are you so silent with me? Are lawyers afraid to talk because they take the law so seriously, because they believe their words might be used as evidence against them?'

'I was just thinking,' he began to relax, and in his head he saw a white canvas chair blowing in the wind. The wind was stiff and the seat of the chair kept slapping itself. 'Maybe I expected too much out of my marriage. Something was missing but maybe that meant something else was there. There never were other women.'

'Was your wife sexy?' She wondered if she would ever be alone in his apartment long enough to look through all his things; she wondered if there were pictures of his wife all over the place, of her, of them, or were they stuck in boxes in the back of a hall closet. She wondered how much of his wife he would want to hold on to.

No answer.

'No, really,' she persisted. 'Was your wife sexy? And don't say no just to please me.'

'No, I can't say she was sexy. Maybe she could have been, but she wouldn't let herself be.' And he realized to himself that she had been even more afraid than he had been.

'Oh, one of those,' Fiarette mumbled. 'Well, what did she do when you made love? Did she get real excited? Did she enjoy every last drop of you?'

'No.'

'Did she ever?'

'I don't think so. She was going to a therapist who told her that premature ejaculation was a man's weapon, the ultimate way he could hold out on a woman, leaving her gasping for more. And that's what she wanted to believe about us. But sex—that part of my life—never seemed that important. All that was important was this—here.' He moved his arms around his office, waved down his law books. 'My wife took care of all the other details, got everything else done. She was . . . so scientific.'

'You don't want scientific, David. Life is all about finding out that what you wanted when you were ten years old, you still want—only bigger.'

And she walked away because her words came to an end.

And she left behind David Pond saying to himself, 'It's been a long time,' and blushing.

And a few days later she was thinking, 'I can't remember the last time I kissed a guy and gave him a hard-on.' But there she was with David Pond doing just that. They had met each other on one level of the building where they worked and had taken an escalator down the next and a ramp down the final until they were walking downtown together. They passed a woodworking shop on lower Fifth Avenue and he told her he'd always wanted a workshop because he loved building things.

And in her apartment she promised him. 'I'm not interested in playing any games. I don't want to be any trouble. I just want to go to bed with you.' She waited for him to say something, but he couldn't. 'Are you sorry you're here?'

'I don't really believe I'm here,' he said. 'I don't really know how I got here.' And then he strung his fingers in her hair and said, 'How do you feel about making love to lawyers?'

'That all depends.'

'On what?'

'On the lawyer.'

She sat back on her bed, palms flat at her sides, and said, 'This is where the magic happens. Do you know how many times I've wanted you here?'

'I've wanted to be here.'

'Really?'

'It went through my mind, sure. I just wasn't sure how to get here.'

Fiarette smiled. There's nothing like that first kiss when you've been waiting so long for it. And she kissed his neck until it rang.

And then they were on the bed and the rest of the words were barely audible.

And two hours later he was still getting used to it.

'You're just what I want, baby,' he said much later. 'Baby?' he repeated. 'I don't think I've ever called a woman "baby" in my whole life.'

'But I bet you always wanted to.'

He smiled and lowered her back into the pillow and even though it was the dead of night she saw sunshine in his eyes.

'What did you mean when you told me in your office that maybe you expected too much out of marriage?'

'I never wanted marriage and I should have stuck with that. You get married because it's time, time to participate. One day my wife said, "Is this the best it will ever be?" We kept waiting for something to happen. We never enjoyed what was going on. You never know what love is all about until much later when you realize what it isn't. But you just keep busy and say nothing. The truth is there was never any pleasure. We never hurt each other but we never helped each other. I never expected anyone to love me, not even her. You know what I mean by love—to work at something the way the word demands. To give more than you've ever given because you find someone who gives you inspiration. Yes, I guess that's it. Love has to be nine parts inspiration. It has to make you feel like you couldn't possibly get what you need anywhere else. Love is like an invitation to something that's hard to get tickets to.'

'I never heard a man talk like that, like passion really counted in his life. Do you think you'll ever get enough?'

'Maybe,' was all he could say. 'What were you like as a child, as a girl?'

'Lonely. I guess all kids are lonely. I lived in a world where I felt like I was rehearsing a scene. I had crushes on everyone I knew although most of them I didn't really know at all. I remember standing at my window when I came home after school when I was in the sixth or seventh grade and watching for this guy Charlie Klein with long black wavy hair come rounding the corner on his way home from high school. I would watch him from wherever I could, but he never noticed me. Once I ripped his name out of his mailbox because that was as close to him as I could get. I just had to have something that was part him. It was written on one side of a macaroni box because on the other side of "Klein" was "Ronzoni". And that was how my emotions went for years. Worship from afar. Kind of like what I felt with you. I guess I'll be getting crushes until the day I die. But they're fun. They make me feel like I'm fourteen years old again.'

'Is that good? Is it good to feel like you're fourteen years old again?'

'You're talking like a lawyer again, David. Why not? Why isn't it good to feel you have it all ahead of you? That's what fourteen years old feels like to me.'

No words for a while.

'Do you get depressed, David?'

'I don't think about it that much,' he said.

'When I get depressed, I always try to think of someone else's life I envy or at least pay attention to, someone who I'd rather be. But the answer is always the same. I don't want to be anyone but me. Maybe it's because I really like being me. I have a reason for everything. I know who I am and how to keep happening. I know how to find out what's going on in more than one place. And it's nice not to envy. Not to need what someone else has unless you can come up with a way to get it for yourself. I never envy anyone anything material.' She stopped and, feeling the bed underneath her, said, 'Talk to me, David. You're not disappointed you're here, are you?' She wondered what she'd do if he said yes, wondered if she looked pretty to him.

He touched her face with the tip of his finger. 'No,' he

smiled, 'and all those times you came into my office and said you couldn't read my handwriting.'

'Yeah. I knew what I was doing. Your handwriting isn't that bad.'

And David Pond started to blush.

'I knew just what I wanted to happen.' And she wet his forehead with her lips. The light made her skin shimmer and she lay against the high circle of the headboard and played with her nipple.

CHAPTER THIRTY

Nabokov said the word 'reality' should never be used
except in quotation marks.

Martin Worthy was feeling the crunch of concentration.
Writing thoughtfully, thoroughly, incisively, was an
exercise in mind elevation; scribbling in space was the
symbol of chaos. And yet each thing had its own
moment.

The biggest mistake a man can make is choosing the
wrong woman, he was thinking, wondering if the man in
his story was afraid of choosing the right woman. Are
there men who turn down women one by one even when
the right ones showed up? Should the character in his
story turn down the woman, too? Or should she turn
him down? How did most encounters get encountered?
Were they just elongated beginnings with nothing really
to become of them, like dead trees? The law of the stars
announces its retirement.

Sometimes when he was writing he felt like being
mean. He wondered why he needed to be so mean
sometimes.

The Cradle of Soaring Cemetery News asked if
anyone was interested in 'purchasing a bench to be
placed near your loved one's final resting place as a
Rememberance.' 'Remembrance' started with a capital

letter and was spelled wrong. Then came a question and answer column.

Question: Why is the funeral important?

Answer: Survivors go through unique kinds of grief. Denial, rage, despondency and acknowledgement. Denial is the most critical one. A traditional funeral with the body present helps the family to understand that someone they loved is dead.

I hated my mother, he thought, because she rarely smiled and I hated my father because he was rarely without a smile. And I hated my wife because she never understood how much I needed to smile. Was life more joy than sadness and was getting over the sadness part of the joy? While he wrote, he smiled. He wished the room was just a little bit warmer. He had to be in the right temperature to create; not feeling precisely comfortable was a distraction. He had to feel just right in order to think beyond himself and into his story. He could have the environment only as a background or have the environment as something the characters could react to. He felt the immeasurable monumental power of the words that were in him. He felt like vice president in charge of mountains. He could make people say anything he wanted to and get away with it.

CHAPTER THIRTY-ONE

Caution: Use of this product may result
in chronic disillusionment with the rest of the world
Ad for a BMW L6 coupé

'Is this a relationship or are we just two people who are sleeping together?'

David and Fiarette were strolling in the Brooklyn Botanic Gardens and she was wondering if he was happy with her breasts. The thought just popped into her mind from nowhere. For a quarter each they went into the hothouse and walked under the powerful mango tree that shimmied all the way up to the hothouse roof. She loved going to bed with him but sometimes he was too fast, like he had the jitters. The whole episode would take a lot of time but he just moved too fast. There was a side room with an entrance that said: 'Please keep this door closed.' Inside was the bonsai collection, and after that the cactus collection, followed by the fern collection. They saw a lady with black hair with two boys who kept running ahead of her, tackling every hill along the way. One of them still wore summer clothes: he was the one who looked into the pond at the Japanese gardens and discovered the giant goldfish and the huge turtle. He yelled to his brother, 'Look at this monster turtle.'

Fiarette told David she thought the lily pads were

'magical', 'Wouldn't it be nice to have a lot of property so if you got depressed you could design a Japanese garden and put in a lily pond? I don't even like flowers all that much but it sounds like a nice idea, some small way out.'

'Out of what? It seems we talk about depressed a lot,' David said.

'That wasn't talking about depressed, that was talking about Japanese gardens. Did your wife talk a lot about being depressed?'

'She didn't know how to talk about it directly, but she would say things like, "David, I know you're going to leave me someday but I hope it will be when I'm strong enough."'

'Women try to get what they need in strange ways sometimes. We all have a modus operandi.' He didn't smile so she assumed it wasn't a joke. 'Did you ever think about leaving her?'

'I didn't think about leaving and I didn't think about staying. I don't think I would have had the guts to leave, even though I knew we would keep gobbling each other's spirit away. Sometimes people exist at the mercy of each other. It's a fact of survival. They say you can learn from wars between countries what we must know in order to restore ourselves as individuals.'

But Fiarette didn't want to talk about wars. 'But you picked her, you chose her.'

'I didn't choose her. So little of life is choice. All of a sudden someone says, "Sign in, please." I chose marriage, I suppose, and then I never had the time to get out of it.'

'I can't imagine staying put if I'm not happy,' Fiarette said.

'You never know.'

'I know. I've defended myself too vigorously all my life. I struggled not to get hurt, left out or left behind. I backed out of closeness because I didn't know how to speak up. People hurt me because they had to; I left them no choice; they did as I suggested. But that didn't stop me from hating them for it so I kept ending things. I hated them because no one could come up with unconditional love. I was always a spoiled brat. One minute it would be a challenge and the next day it would be a pushover.'

'So you like to call the shots.'

'I guess that's one way of putting it. Control is an advanced passion of mine. I like to be able to do the forecasting. But then you get stuck with a year like this one, when so many things come down that you could never have guessed at, never have projected, never have stored enough understanding for. Why do you think there are years like that, so full of motion, so full of tragedy, of change, of promise, but not always purpose? And other times three or four years go by and it feels like nothing is going on.'

'Maybe it's all in the stars.'

'David, do you need a woman in your life?'

He looked at her but had no real answer.

'Because I need something that's mine and the only way that can be is if someone really needs me.'

She wondered if maybe he never needed a woman, would never need a woman. 'Did she and you fight a lot? What makes you really realize a marriage is over—when you fight too much or you fight too little?'

'We were too tired to fight.'

'Can't you talk about it more?'

'At first it was something to protect, to hold on to, a challenge; and then you get wise and begin to wonder why everyone pushes to make a lousy marriage work.'

'That's what I wonder—why force two people to get along.' She made a face and wished she had a piece of gum, preferably Chiclets, cinnamon Chiclets. 'Anger is the most honest emotion,' she said.

'Who told you that?'

'I just decided.'

'After we got married, I lived in a house where I craved attention, maybe not every minute, but certainly for most of the years. Hers was the kind of denial that leaves you with no illusions at all. I wanted to feel like a man.'

'Maybe you needed to be meaner. Maybe you were feeling too charitable.' Her voice changed to now. 'Do you think good things can happen to us? How do you know the same thing won't happen between you and me that happened between you and her?'

'I have no idea what will happen between us. But with me and her—nothing happened between me and her. That's what happened—nothing happened and then she killed herself. It wasn't something that happened between us. The word "between" doesn't belong there.'

'You sound like you had nothing to do with it.'

'I'm not sure I did.'

'How can that be? If she was happy, she would have . . . something like that would never have happened.'

'Fiarette . . .' he began.

'Don't say something that will hurt me.'

'Fiarette, the trouble is women are always more romantic than men. They see intrigue where there isn't any.'

'That's because men are afraid of romance.'

'They're not afraid. They're just made different.'

'Do you think your wife knew about me?'

'What was there to know?'

'Women know that something's going on before it ever does. That's how they're different.'

He smiled.

'Didn't you think months ago that something might happen between us?'

'I told you I thought about it.'

'Before or after my note?'

'Why do you have so many questions?'

'Because I want to know.'

CHAPTER THIRTY-TWO

'Wide shoulders are the flared trousers of the eighties.'
David Bowie

At work Fiarette was looking through notes for her word processor, notes she had started keeping a year ago about things she still failed to understand: For instance, the table of authorities a/k/a 'The DOTS Program'. 'To revise dots, see what character is at the last word and put a tab two spaces after this and a tab at 87 and put periods in and stop when the character # changes.' She had no idea what she was thinking of when she wrote it. Did she really ever want to conquer the DOTS program? Every time an attorney asked her to put dots in a table of authorities, she had a reason for him why the dots part really wasn't necessary. She managed nicely to stay on the slopes of credibility. More notes: 'Code 3 name and address switch code, code 2.' She tossed that and more into the wastebasket. She hated her job more and more. She began to worry that David was an ingenious inspiration to make life more bearable. Today a memorandum had been circulated to all word processors that a whole new system was being introduced; new machines, new magic, were coming into the office, new garbled essence. She had been using the other one for a year, was still learning it, and did not welcome the risks of something new. But you can't sue somebody for a dirty trick. A few days later the new machines started coming out of cartons all over the place and being set up with laser printers. Every other day after that a new note was stuck up on the wall about a feature that had been discovered on the PC or a trick on how to do things faster and safer as the machine oriented word processing operators (everyone but her) dug deep into the intriguing transition. Machines had a way of trying to outdo themselves. The competition they had with themselves was fearsome. It was one more reason not to like them. Just because you say thank you to God doesn't mean you're going to get more. Everyone got new folders, pink ones, to keep the new notes for the new machines. For Fiarette the notes held the intellectual mystery of a traffic jam. High concepts were fragile temples. She had no choice but to study the machine every day, practicing things like:

> control arrow right moves word by word;
> control arrow left moves word by word;
> home home arrow down takes you to the top of a
> document
> 'go to' plus arrow right or arrow left will move you
> in the columns program
> escape plus arrow down will move you any number
> of lines you instruct

She typed exercises that read like this:

> Bears have been searching for left over pizza in
> campgrounds since the tourist season started.

The day after she typed the lesson about the hungry

bears she found in her mailbox an ad for a new book called *Working Couples*. It listed some topics that would be addressed in the book: pre-nuptial agreements; reading the annual report together; is your household under–capitalized; who should own what; the liabilities of co-signing; and, finally, divorce, resources and you.

And the next morning she went back to work and started all over again with a typing exercise on the importance of being able to identify Christmas trees that can be legally harvested.

This was followed by a lesson about columns: 'Columns have special tabs; they can be L for left, R for right, D for decimal.'

And at eleven a.m. another memorandum from the word processing coordinator that ended with a warning:

> Be absolutely sure you have the correct back-up disc and be resolutely sure you follow this procedure with EVERY SINGLE document you handle. Failure to follow this procedure has resulted in problems, frustration and extra work for word processing and the attorneys. Until we can link the microcomputers in word processing, adherence to the above procedure in vital.

All those demands and they spelled 'is' wrong in the last line.

In the middle of all this common ground, love happened. Not only did it happen, but it grew. A fatal thickening and the frills of adoration.

Martin Worthy wasn't certain his plot was coherent, but the direction was smooth and the labels were permanent. He had to please both sides: himself and the crowds. Skilled mimicry with a few headstands. He had to use the words mercy and vulnerable. Leisure America (you'll love it too much to leave it) was blowing in the wind. Everybody would have a chance to be there but on the way things would be double-bagged; some people would get hurt and some people would run. No one is harmless, but there are many meaningless harbors and no one pays attention to ice cold solutions.

He held his fingers steady on the pencil, a trigger, reminding him he must stay in control. The words came but they drifted; they had no backup. No bark. And he wondered what more needed to be said. The book was almost finished now and it was time to wrap up those words that had howled for creation in the first place, those people who had stirred up struggles with the confident allure of a new mask.

Some mornings, to be sure, he would be more consumed by whether he should have a corn muffin or a buttered sesame. Or he would waste time with the mail that might arrive with some news from the cemetery where he would learn that: 'For the first time ever, two (2) years interest free on mausoleum space purchased from April first to May thirty-first only. Since you showed an interest in the past, we feel an obligation to keep you informed.'

But he was always delighted when he recognized what it was like to get to know a person who had a story to tell, to let him fly, clip his wings if need be, crumble his details, but always, always give him a chance to speak up for himself, because he just might end up telling you what to do. His eyes moistened. Writing was an exceptional cup of coffee.

Martin put the pencil down. He didn't know where that last line had come from. He was off beyond the groove thinking of other things while the words got said. It felt like his characters no longer needed him. They were experiencing the first signs of glowing pleasures, the lights of a great big city coming on at night. He was left behind thinking about canned loneliness. What do people really do when they talk? What do they do between words? Where do their eyes go? Where do their hands go? Whose shadows do they look at? If they have to sneeze, how long do they wait? What do people do with yesterday's newspapers? What do they do with yesterday?

CHAPTER THIRTY-THREE

In *The Lonely Lady* by Harold Robbins:
'Love is what each individual person thinks it is.
Love is what two people agree it is.
And it is different for every person who loves.'

At work Fiarette had lunch with a new girl, a temp, who said, 'Do you know one of the best things in life is Kellogg's Variety Pack? It makes breakfast so easy and . . . versatile.'

'Versatile?' Fiarette said to her head. Versatile. A *versatile* breakfast. Somehow it wasn't level.

'I discovered Kellogg's Variety Pack when I was on Weight Watchers. You can have three quarters of an ounce of cereal every day—Rice Krispies happened to be exactly three quarters of an ounce but a little box of Raisin Bran was one and a half, and I just decided they would even themselves out. You can only have about three teaspoons of Grape Nuts—they weigh a lot, but I like them because they're crunchy so I don't mind having less. I used to spend all day trying to decide if I should count the cereal as a bread exchange or a protein exchange and try to keep my fruits down to three small ones.'

Fiarette saw him wherever she looked; she kept getting caught up in his face. He was part of her day. Love was created to keep peace, the precious window of diligence.

Halloween was coming up. She remembered the red beret Kary had worn last year when they went to the Greenwich Village parade. She recalled so much of the past, but her memories lacked intimacy; the past was no more than a fact. She thought mostly about now and what would happen next. David wasn't a game to her and that was the big difference this time, the desire for genuine restoration. Outside the clock was seven minutes slow.

'What are you thinking about, Fiarette?' asked the girl who sat across from her at lunch.

'Nothing.'

What she was thinking was I wonder if he's afraid he'll get to mean too much to me. Maybe I should ask him next time I see him. If there is a next time. What if he says yes? What if he's had enough of me? Then I'll have to talk myself out of loving him.

That night she wondered if washing her hair every day would dry it out. But she did it anyway. Once a day habits were easier for her to remember than once a week ones or three times a week ones.

That same night David looked into the mirror in the bedroom he had once shared with a wife. In the reflection he saw flowered wallpaper, a leaded glass desk lamp and the face of a man who was shocked that he felt so remote from it all. Death had been an invasion and yet so significantly ordinary. He did not mourn because he did not feel mournful. He felt full of love and death at the same time, abandoning his consciousness to dead words and then reviving it with the image of Fiarette, her full lips that went from gentle surprise to tender amusement. Death and love. Love for the living, love for the ones who get stuck behind. A stomping ground. Love: necessary, connective tissue, high priests and musical profiles. How he needed it suddenly. How he would do anything for it, make any sacrifice; how sad he felt that he had gone so long without it. She had made him swoon. It was nothing less. 'Where'd you learn to make love like that?' he had asked her and she had spun a smile at him. 'Desire.'

Was it love? Was it enough like love to pass for it? Would it stay put? Would that be sufficient?

He thought of last night and he could see her now, standing there, rubbing perfume oil on her wrists, her temples, sitting on the edge of the bed, dangling her legs. 'Did you love her?' she had wanted to know. 'She was my wife,' he said.

'That's not what I asked you. Did you love her—did you share all the things lovers share—did you get drunk on white wine and sit on each other's laps; did you go for walks in the park and ask a stranger to take a picture of the two of you under a beautiful pink dogwood tree?'

He hadn't wanted to be honest. He hadn't wanted to say no, damn it, I didn't love her. We didn't do those kinds of things. I didn't feel like it. I couldn't feel like it. She used to grab a Kleenex every time we made love and wipe my come from between her legs. No sooner was it there than she wanted it gone. He thought of all these things but kept them to himself. He didn't want her to know how uninteresting it had really been.

'Love is attraction by design,' Fiarette had told him once. He thought of her words now: a trend, a wave, a phase. Outside in the street someone was sitting in a car playing the reggae radio station. It was the sort of night where any kind of music would have fit in.

Do I need to love or to be loved? Suppose I can't have both? Which is more important?

'Everyone knows that men lie,' Fiarette had announced to him quite regally one day while she peeled off her nail polish. 'The question is what do they lie about most. Other women? Other men? Illusion? Confusion? Humility? Futility? I wonder about lies and truths all the time.'

And now David Pond wondered what, after all, was going on?

CHAPTER THIRTY-FOUR

'A line is a dot that went for a walk.'
Paul Klee

Martin Worthy did not want any of these words, these figurines in his mind, to come to an end. He did not want to interrupt the reward. He had chosen this work, the strict enchantment, this book, over all living things. The experience of the sweaty smile. The strategy of purpose. This book that would speak about the humanity of attachment, a glimpse at an insurgent in sympathy with an army. Writing shifted the attachment.

Now he was even closer to being finished and he would have to return to reality. Life is a crime story, a resurrected legend, eager claims and mounting virtues. Life is the glamour of tradition. If I cannot write, I cannot exist. What will I do with my time? What will I do with the things I am afraid of? Where will I hide them? Where will I hide from them? Love is too terrible, too temporary; it only works in books. The writer can make love happen to everyone but himself. I have never felt as comfortable with any human being as I have with a pad of yellow legal paper. I have never been myself with other people. No one. Even my best friends were still too far away. It was always so delicious to be alone.

If you look at yourself only in the dark, you can be anybody you want.

Fiarette was starting to feel the fire in David's voice, the vague poetics. His voice had lacked the warmth of a lover. But he found himself talking vigorously about miniature dilemmas that until now had existed only inside his head. 'My brother didn't have time to mourn my mother's death; he was already married and his first son was born just two months after she died. Birth takes the place of death. It doesn't take people long to get used to good news and whoever died yesterday just gets buried deeper. Life is really subtle when we play it that way.'

She hung on to his every word and when he didn't sleep with her she slept on the side of her bed that had become his, bundling herself up against the pillow.

And one Sunday afternoon they walked to the East Village and saw an artist on St Mark's Place who was selling color xeroxes of his paintings. Pictures of girls dancing, acrobats turning, stairs winding and people sliced in two. He bought her one of Jim Morrison for three dollars. Jim's face was white and seamless, haunting. She had loved it. Sid and Nancy was two fifty. And then she bought herself a copy of *Rat Subterranean News* from 1969 for one dollar from a guy with no teeth and dirty hair. There was a story on Vietnam and something called 'Long Hair Loose in Cuba'. And an ad for a bookstore on Avenue C: 'The peace eye bookstore where chromosome-damaged Maoists lead pregnant coeds from the Bronx down the dope-strewn path to the dissolution of western civilization. Poetry. Peace. Revolution.' There was an ad for strobe lights from Zipcom Corp. in Little Rock, Arkansas. And 'Magical

Mystery Tour' was playing at Philharmonic Hall in Lincoln Center and all seats cost three dollars. There was an ad for Stella cigarette papers in banana, strawberry, cherry, mint, licorice and chocolate. In the front it said: 'Black market automatic rifles going for about $65. The time to arm yourself is now.'

They walked into Tompkins Square Park and watched a puppy named Shadow fooling around with a bulldog. And Fiarette gathered up some leaves, red ones, yellow ones with strikes of green, and carried them home in her pockets.

CHAPTER THIRTY-FIVE

Paul Newman to Patricia Neal, as Alma, in *Hud*:
'I'll remember you, honey. You're the one that got away.'

For a moment David Pond let himself remember that Fiarette was the first woman he had ever wanted a picture of. He knew which picture he wanted, too; he had seen it at her apartment, her standing on the beach, close up of her face, smiling and wet. He didn't know what he'd do with it; he thought he would probably pin it up in the bathroom so he could see it while he was shaving. It was raining now and he realized he drank more coffee when it rained; he wondered if she did, too.

And Fiarette was thinking that what she really wanted, silent movies and a twenty-four hour a day attachment, was not at all likely. Hers was a humble alliance with hopeless limits. And David suddenly thought that the notion of wanting her picture was rather crazy after all. He laughed at how naive he had become; he had wanted all the good parts underlined twice, but that only made everything else less clear.

The next time she saw him she heard herself say, 'It's not that I took this whole relationship seriously. It's just that it's starting to become significant. Like an outside threat.'

'Well,' he countered, 'I guess I've been thinking

something like that myself, that maybe we were getting too attached.'

She was surprised. He wasn't supposed to agree. 'I wonder which one of us will feel like we've been left behind. Whoever gets left over is the one who took it more seriously. Love never happens in equal parts.'

He smiled but not that much.

'You don't have to sweet talk me, David. I'm out to get laid.'

'You shouldn't talk like that. Men don't enjoy being sexual objects. It forces them to make decisions about who to pursue and who to stay away from.'

'I think it's a little late to be telling me that. Are you trying to say I've been doing the wrong thing all along?' She was sorry that she had spoiled him by telling him how good he was in bed. She was sorry that she had ever made him feel like a man.

'Oh, Fiarette, it's wearing me out.'

'Sex?'

'No, no, you, us, this whole thing, whatever it is. No, no, not sex. I didn't mean anything like that.' His face softened. He was remembering how nice the hair between her legs smelled.

'Maybe we ought to just forget it, David. I need spontaneity.'

'There you go again, calling bad habits survival mechanisms.'

'Is that what you think of me? I'll tell you what I think of you. You get mad at yourself if you're sleepy and you get anxious when you're wide awake. You never learned how to talk life over with the rest of the world. You keep it all to yourself and then you take it out on me. You never want to talk about things while they're going on.'

'I'm not much of a talker.'

'Why?'

'It saves me from making a fool of myself.'

'Are you trying to say I'm making a fool of myself?'

'I'm trying to say my biggest disappointment is in myself for being intimidated by people who didn't even know what the word meant.'

'What does that have to do with me?'

'Not everything has something to do with you.'

'Suppose I need it to?'

'Then maybe you really are better off alone. Or maybe it's me. Maybe I'm the one who's better off alone.' His voice tried to be final.

Out in the street someone yelled, 'You don't have a chance, motherfucker.'

She felt tears in her eyes. The tears streaming down her face had a peculiar warmth. 'I just realized I'm not interested anymore in what makes things work. Only that they do work. I want windows that let sunlight in and a t.v. that goes on and off and soap that doesn't blotch my skin and a life as simple as possible.'

'Maybe I'd better go.'

'Go, but don't think you'll ever get to know who I am, David.' She wondered if she gave in to herself too much of the time.

That night David Pond visited his aunt. She was eighty-three and it was the first time he had ever seen her walking with a cane. He wondered if sometimes it wasn't better to be dead than old and sick. He wondered what time meant to old people. If you asked them, 'Did you have a nice weekend?' would they answer, 'When was it?' From the look of things, did they know that winter was really here?

Fiarette decided that night that a lot of people live like

they're frozen. Frozen beyond distraction. Life was a whole different job for them. Life was massive unrepaired defeat.

At work the next day she had lunch with a woman whose husband had died a year ago after a heart attack; he weighed close to three hundred pounds. Now she had a boyfriend who was twelve years younger which made him eight years older than her daughter.

Fiarette picked at her mushrooms and smothered some more house dressing on them. She thought of David, how he wrote out shopping lists and abbreviated everything. T.P. was toilet paper. She missed him and she hadn't even gotten used to the fact that he was gone. Her lunch companion was telling her how she had met her new boyfriend. 'It had been raining all day and the volley ball game turned out to be drinks instead. We ended up in the back seat of his car and he wanted to come home with me. But my daughter was there.'

'And what if she wasn't?'

'Well, sure, why not?' She buttered a piece of the roll that wasn't hers. Fiarette thought about folding a piece of mushroom in a ribbon of spinach.

And David was two floors below in his office, thinking about how beautiful she always looked minutes after he had made love to her, her cheeks full with the rush of her own blood, her eyes burning landscapes. And how a few weeks ago at four o'clock in the afternoon she had delivered work to his office and said, 'Why don't you fuck me?' That's when she looked the best of all—when she asked him. Spiced. He thought of his marriage: mutually assured destruction was the best he could do with figuring out a name for it. Mutually assured destruction must have been what we both needed at the time. We are where we need to be.

And Fiarette sat at the PC, known as Machine No. 4, and read her notes:

> Block must be on to highlight in order to bold.
> Backslash OVR is where the machine saves back-up material.

She was concerned with deconstruction and the need to feel close to someone. There was no more contentment to being a lonely animal. What else do you feel besides hungry? She did not want to become a gloomy legend. Loneliness has nothing to do with how many people you know.

She tried to forget herself by doing a spellcheck on a document she was working on. Spell check—hit save first (F10); then spell (red F2). Spellcheck was a PC feature that would check the spelling of a page or of an entire document and ask you questions which you could choose to: '1. Skip, 2. Ignore, or 3. Edit.' She never understood the difference between 'skip' and 'ignore'. Most of the time it was pretty helpful, like when it knew 'suficient' should be 'sufficient' 'poayment' should be 'payment' and 'tghe' should be 'the'. But if you typed something like EPE4NSES the machine guessed at what you wanted and its guesses went like this:

PE	EPA
APO	OP
YAP	YAWP
AP	EPEE
UPI	YIP

And it had no idea that if you typed 'sek' you might want 'seek'. It suggested:

SEC	STK
SEW	SAX
SACK	SAUCE
PSYCHE	SEX

And she wanted to cry because of the way things are, always a tragedy going on. But what really hurt her was the trouble she was having finding something to be grateful for. She thought of a line in a song by Styx: 'I have nothing to do and all day to do it.'

That night David found himself dialing a telephone.
    'Don't you know I've fallen in love with you?'
    'Really?'
    'You saved my life.'
    She was grinning.
    'I didn't think you loved me as much as you used to,' she said to him, 'and then I realized how could that be—we just met each other.'   •
    And if you were looking through the window into her apartment scarcely an hour later, you would have seen a pair of jeans get flung up in the air and sail across a room, followed by some raucous dogged laughter.

CHAPTER THIRTY-SIX

'Somebody still cares about quality.'
Budweiser

Fiarette woke up alone on a Sunday morning thinking of David Pond. All year long he worked more weekends than he took off. Who was he? All she knew about him was (1) he was a lawyer and (2) his wife had just died.

She got tired of staring at the walls and sat down and read through her journal. Back six months, forward four months, back ten weeks, forward ten days.

'I love my hair. It is getting longer and I love the way it feels. The longer it gets, the happier I am. I HAVE NO INTENTION OF EVER GETTING IT CUT.'

'I have been to bed with two men this week. Wednesday night Mike from the gym and tonight Charles from Jane Street. Both times I was thinking of David Pond (a lawyer at work). How I'd like to lick the sweat off him. I should just go up to him and say "let's do it.*"' At the bottom of the page she had another*: 'To be continued.'

His name or something about him was all over the place:

'I had a dream that David Pond moved in with me.'

'Mike from the gym called and said it was "delicious" and we ought to "do it every week". I keep thinking about David Pond and how every man smells different.'

'Emotions make me lazy. I cannot seem to do and to feel at the same time. When I feel, everything else stops.'

'I feel sick as a dog. All I want to do is sleep. Maybe I'm dying.'

'I am amazed at how involved I let my emotions get. David Pond. I know I sound like an adolescent, but I can't help it. He hardly knows I'm alive but I'm already jealous of his secretary.'

More and more was about David Pond:

'I want to have an affair. I really do. I want him like crazy. I am always in heat.'

'He looks at me and my heart stands still.'

'I haven't been happy for a long time. That's why I have to fill this journal up with good things, so I can thumb through them years from now looking for happy words.'

'The excitement begins anew. I want to eat him up. Dilemma, dilemma.'

'I am on the verge of tears. I sort of have been for three days now. Is it physical or mental? I never ever know.'

Then after she and David started going to bed:

'I dwell on him.'

'I never seem to sleep the whole night through. Always seem to wake up or to be awakened. I'm not sure which.'

'I feel incredible stress. How much money I spend. How much I save. Where it all goes. When I'll die. If I'm eating the best that I can. If I should eat cheaper. If David will want me. Why the shampoo I like is so expensive. How not to waste it. How to make my hair stay curled. Why I can't sleep the whole night through. I'm in a bad mood.'

David. God, she shuddered. She had him but there

was nothing there. He had not come from anyplace. He was just beginning to come out of the shadows but he wasn't sure who he wanted to portray. Experience was up against character and his was a varying optimism. He was hardly emotionally equipped to deal with all those options. She was frantic with a sense of his irrelevance.

She put on her long black flared coat and went for a walk.

The words inside Martin Worthy could scarcely wait their turn to get on paper. He knew what had to be done. His story was ready for an ending. The finishing touch was two final sentences, each one in its own paragraph.

'Everybody should get a chance to ride off into the sunset once in his life.'

'And so they did.'

Outside it was cold but Martin wanted to get some air. This would be his first Christmas without Elsa; he had no one to shop for and the apartment felt crowded. On the street his feet crushed a 'Step into Wilderness' button.

He sat on a bench in the park and opened his notebook.

He hadn't seen her since that Christmas party, and maybe one more time right after that Christmas party, but there she was: the girl with the red hair, her hands in the big square pockets of a long black flared coat. She was strolling into the park and slowed up as she walked past him, and smiled.

'I'm writing a book,' he said when she noticed his notebook. He was really sitting there unable to come up with a single thought and considering sketching a squirrel half way up a tree.

'Is it about love?' she wanted to know.

'Isn't everything?' He smiled and knew he liked her.

'Love is the biggest mystery of all,' Fiarette said. She was constantly thinking about love and always ready to talk about it.

'What makes you say that?'

'Because it's hard to know when it's real.'

'Love is just knowing how to care for someone even when they let you down.'

'I certainly don't feel that way about him at all,' she said with an air of ready acceptance.

'Does he feel that way about you?'

'I don't think he would even understand what we're talking about.'

She stopped talking and was struck again that David couldn't possibly mean everything when she was so taken by this stranger, this man with eyes the color of walnuts. With no scarf and no hat, only gloves. David was always so bundled up, always afraid of catching a cold. This stranger with shoes that weren't shined. David's shoes were always shined. David didn't have a dirty anything. Rational respect was the worst kind: he didn't know how to do anything wrong. His world was writing things like: 'Resolved, that the President and Vice President of the Corporation be and each hereby is,' and then changing it to read: 'Resolved, that the President and Vice President of the Corporation, acting singly, be and each hereby is. . . .'

Somehow this man whom she barely knew, who stood inches away from her, made her feel warm, a rhythm, a bountiful, blissful rhythm.

'How will I know when your book comes out?'

'If you give me your phone number, I'll call you and tell you all about it.'

She gave him her phone number and they both knew he would call her up in a week at the most.

That night she went home and wrote in her journal something about this all being 'part of the road to priorities' and how 'action takes the place of sinking needs'. And something about getting stronger.

She wasn't even sure whether she wanted to see David again, let alone love him. Some people get dangerous when they get mobilized. David's life was full of writing paragraphs called 'Distribution of Profits', changing words like 'assessment' to 'analogy' or phrases like 'governing export control' to 'regarding export control', dealing with dates as far away as September 1 in the year 2010. She found one of his marked up drafts that she had saved just to bring a piece of him home with her and laughed at it.

She wondered if the man in the park bought his wife Valentine's Day presents. She wondered if David would even send her a Valentine's Day card. And then she knew she was no longer terrifically in love with David Pond and whether or not he sent her a card on Valentine's Day didn't matter. She had seen too many people die: another Valentine's Day more or less didn't matter. What mattered was the dignity of not having to make believe, the reward of decency, a stately poem called sweetness, and flirting with new back-up vocals.

I could be comfortable in your arms, she was thinking about the man in the park. Life was about to begin again.

CHAPTER THIRTY-SEVEN

Seems Like Old Times

It was time for Kate and Teddy's annual Christmas party.

The parchment woodwork needed to be repainted, but Martin's Paint Store had gone out of business and Fay's Drug Store had taken its place. There were a few new things on the walls: a maroon and mint green sign 'Hasta La Victoria Siempre' and nearby a black and white photograph of an apple tree in blossom she had taken in May in the mountains. They had bought three pillows in Bloomingdale's covered in a pattern called 'Coney Island Madness'. But everything else was pretty much the same.

Andy decided to skip the Christmas party that year. His ex-wife Shelly had managed to get invited first. Shelly wasn't in love with Andy anymore, but she sure as hell wasn't about to surrender him totally. Other women were beginning to notice him now that he was single again and she didn't like that at all. Denise and Tom had decided not to live with each other anymore. His snoring was keeping her awake too many nights. But they both decided to come to the party, separately. Yet later that night he would tell her, and anyone else who wanted to listen, that he fell in love with her because she was always trying to make him laugh.

Randy was telling Maggie that the first thing you cut out when you have no money is sugar and milk. Then he told her that on the subway he had seen a poster of Tammy Fay Bakker and someone had rubber stamped it 'Find a Cure'. And Maggie had remembered that last summer on the day there was an earthquake in Los Angeles she was thinking about buying a pony tail clip and that was the day she met Randy at the Indian store on St Mark's Place. And the following week while her husband's plane was on its way to Madrid, she was on her way to have Indian food in the East Village with her new lover whose wife was in Block Island at a family reunion. And the Springer sisters were talking about their new real estate venture they would call 'Spring'.

I hope I don't turn out to be obnoxious, someone was heard to be saying, I know I'm going through so many changes.

Fiarette wasn't at this year's Christmas party. She was in her kitchen with the aroma of chicken in the oven. She bent over to face her knees and then some more, touching her toes, her palms brushing the terracotta floor. Through her legs she could see the oak chair upside down in the next room bathed in winter sunshine. She giggled at the suggestion of being upside down, recalling the breathless delight at being swung around as a child, her legs planted firmly around her favorite uncle's waist, or being on a swing, stretched back on the downside, the world at a different pace, with no need to edit the music. She asked herself what the year had been about and could come up only with this. It was about being kinder in a clumsy world, holding your head up when it haunts you with its dialogue, being sweet when it teases you with its power, having faith when it strips away the love songs. Here, another year later, she realized she could remember the day of the week that Alex had died, the moment of Kary's parting, the first time David had kissed her, and the afternoon she and Martin Worthy had moved toward each other in the park.

And, for now, way outside dilemma, away from life's temporary island where everyone was going through a change of ownership, feeling a natural symmetry of enriched but dependent reflections, she smiled.